One Sore Rib

One Sore Rib

Matthew Cooper McLean

NEW PULP PRESS

Published by New Pulp Press, LLC, 926 Truman Avenue, Key West, Florida 33040, USA.

One Sore Rib copyright © 2017 by Matthew Cooper McLean. Electronic compilation/ paperback edition copyright © 2017 by New Pulp Press, LLC. Cover photography by Matthew C. McLean, Cover design by The Zen Orange (thezenorange.com).

All rights reserved. No part of this book may be reproduced, scanned, or transmitted in any form or by any means, electronic or mechanical, including photocopying, recording, or any information storage and retrieval system, without permission in writing from the publisher. Please do not participate in or encourage piracy of copyrighted materials in violation of the author's rights. Purchase only authorized ebook editions.

This is a work of fiction. Names, characters, places, and incidents either are the product of the author's imagination or are used fictitiously, and any resemblance to actual persons, living or dead, businesses, companies, events, or locales is entirely coincidental. While the author has made every effort to provide accurate information at the time of publication, neither the publisher nor the author assumes any responsibility for errors, or for changes that occur after publication. Further, the publisher does not have any control over and does not assume any responsibility for author or third-party websites or their contents. How the ebook displays on a given reader is beyond the publisher's control. For information contact:
Publisher@NewPulpPress.com

ISBN-13: 978-1945734151 (New Pulp Press)
ISBN-10: 1945734159

Printed in the United States of America
Visit us on the web at www.newpulppress.com

This isn't an accurate depiction of anything.

One
Sore Rib

CHAPTER 1

She was an old man's whore who didn't speak a lick of English. It was clear that I had woken her up, but even with her hair a mess, no makeup, and her eyes puffy from not enough sleep or too much drink the night before, she was beautiful. Beautiful, young and tall, at least half a hand taller than me, which wasn't intimidating for a reason I've never been able to nail down.

The alleyway into the Venice apartment building was narrow, gray, and mostly shadowed in the light of that autumn morning. If this had been America, nobody would have opened the sturdy wooden door to an outsider banging on it. Especially a cold, hungry, and hungover one wanting to get inside with the pitiful breakfast I had managed to scrounge up. But she did, and not by a timid crack, but all the way like she was about to confront my screaming mess, tell me to shut up and go away. Then she recognized me as a fellow tenant, having passed me on the spiral staircase that wrapped itself around the central elevator shaft, leaving no room for mistaken identity when you squeezed by others.

I gestured in an attempt to get across that I had forgotten my keys in what I hoped was something of a universal language. She just motioned me in, twirling her hand at the end of her wrist and waggling her head, understanding enough and not caring about the details, twittering away in friendly, dense, and completely indecipherable Italian. The elevator was used mostly for baggage and, like all things Venetian, was too cramped and slow for the American in me, so I thanked her a few times and started up the stairs to the third floor. To my surprise and discomfort, she followed me.

The stone stairs echoed our footsteps and her stream of Italian as we walked up. I responded to the latter with a more extensive and bumbling explanation of having left my keys in the apartment I was renting with my wife. I used the word 'wife' defensively, which usually worked to scare off women that I found myself attracted to. Cheryl was going about the business of dying and had chosen to do so in Venice. And in that lonely cold box that was Venice in autumn, with its ancient stone buildings, dirty canals and rainclouds, I didn't want to complicate things with an extramarital affair. I hadn't made it through nine years of marriage to break her heart at the end.

When we reached my door I didn't have any choice but to bang on it and yell for Cheryl as the inner door, like its outside counterpart, locked automatically when it closed. As I shouted, hoping she would have the strength that morning to answer, my blonde companion hovered behind me, tittering quietly to herself, obviously amused at my percussional entry dance. I had half forgotten she was there, wondering what contingency plan I had if Cheryl didn't wake. Could I climb to the roof and get in through the balcony?

Almost completely hairless now, gaunt and pale, but with much of her beauty untouched, wrapped in a pearl colored sarong, Cheryl answered the door. She was as bleary-eyed as my escort, halfway through a sentence telling me to stop making so much noise when she noticed the other woman. Her surprise didn't chase all of the sleep away, but she smiled, looking past while speaking to me, "Who's your friend?"

I 'oh'ed and 'uhm'ed for a second, not sure how to

explain bringing home a local girl. The girl in question used the moment to step forward and extend her hand to Cheryl as if she were introducing herself for a job interview – perfect posture, eyes bright, arm straight. Another stream of Italian came out, out of which I caught that her name was Sophie. Cheryl smiled, took Sophie's hand, and quickly, politely, and in perfect Italian introduced me and her. For what must have been the fiftieth time I kicked myself for letting my wife convince me to come to the one place where it seemed like I was the only one who didn't speak the language.

To my surprise, Cheryl invited her in. She had very little energy these days, spending most of it on the couch, so the generous social gesture took me aback. But Sophie strolled right in, seemingly pleased with the invitation. We commenced a nickel tour, starting with the largest room (the living room) and proceeded vertically through the ever-shrinking rooms, ending with the smallest, the roof garden. To call it a garden was an insult to my mother's. Hers was expansive and held a variety of plants while this one would barely cover a postage stamp, really just a deck with potted plants. But it was tall enough to overlook the stacked and jutting roofs of Venice.

Cheryl sat down at the table in the center of the deck, putting her elbow on the wooden, warped surface, tilting her head into her stick-like hand, giving both of us a weary smile. Sophie walked the perimeter of the garden, spouting what sounded like very positive, enthusiastic things as she gazed out over the city. I think at some point she may have said, "You can even see the ocean," but I can't be sure. I was trying not to care that it was nice to have someone around with that much energy. She only stopped when she turned back to face us and realized Cheryl was asleep.

With a sympathetic coo, Sophie walked over and

bent to examine her, then turned to me with questioning eyes. Not knowing how to explain 'cancer' and 'terminal' I could only shrug. I didn't see the point in sharing the darkness we had brought with us, but it was clear that Sophie had some idea of what was happening when she placed a gentle hand on Cheryl's cheek. The ability to feel for others was something that they shared in common.

I eventually announced that the visit was over the only way I could. I picked up Cheryl (my knees buckled for the millionth time at feeling her reduced weight) and walking down the stairs to set her on the couch in the living room. Sophie followed, quiet as a child sneaking downstairs on Christmas Eve, but without all that pesky joy.

When I finished laying her out on the couch and Cheryl hadn't woke up, Sophie made quiet questioning noises, which I dismissed with hand gestures as I watched my wife. But then Cheryl blinked awake and made what sounded like an apology. Sophie smiled and waved, like people do to babies behind the glass at maternity wards, and turned to leave. This time I looked towards her and, despite all of the guilt in my dirty little soul, I couldn't help but watch her go. Her beauty had set me back before, but now that she was leaving, I assumed forever, I could take a moment and drink it in. With her facing away from me and my wife behind me, I did so without fear of reproach and only my own conscious to hassle me.

Cheryl said, "She seems nice. We should invite her over sometime."

"She doesn't speak English." I said absently as I watched Sophie disappear over the threshold of the last home my wife would ever know.

"Maybe I could teach her," Cheryl said

I watched her hips swing out the door.

"Yeah."

Chapter 2

Cheryl, in her own way, had already become a ghost.

In the beginning there was plenty to keep us busy, in frightened, double-quick time. There were oncologist visits to go to, appointments to make, advice to be sought, articles to read, surgeries to plan, and the poison of chemotherapy sessions. Like a quarterback learning a new playbook, I became very familiar with cancer very quickly; its conventional treatments, its alternative treatments, and how it bends and twists your own cells and genetics to eat away at you. The disease has its own black bible and I wouldn't encourage anyone to become familiar with it unless their need is great.

It was during those early days that I learned the simple but inescapable fact that someone with Cheryl's type of cancer (a particularly nasty, vicious, and aggressive breed of what I came to think of as the Beast) had little chance of survival. Slim to none. But Death wasn't knocking at the door right then. It was just a black figure on the horizon and you learn to live with it. As the scars of surgery healed and the regimen of chemotherapy started, little by little I watched my wife, a beautiful shining woman, dim and dim until there was just a shell of her that rarely left the couch. Even then I was sure, with a certainty that I can't explain, that Cheryl would bounce back with the buoyancy that only Cheryl seemed to possess, and kick the Beast in the tail and order Death back to his distant horizon.

But there's that final hospital visit, the one where they can't look you in the eye, the one that makes the doctor feel like a failure and makes you want to kill

One Sore Rib

him for it. But you clench your fists and tell yourself it's not his fault as he informs you that the treatments aren't working, that the tumors have kept growing, and there's nothing left that they can do. Go home, make yourself comfortable. Or as the samurai used to say, "Wash your neck and wait."

Cheryl being Cheryl, though, said, "Fuck that." The declaration that her death was inevitable, even imminent, gave her a burst of energy – there were places she had never seen, things she had never done and it was time to squeeze some of those in. In a short time we visited Alaska to see the Aurora Borealis, went to China to see the Great Wall, to Australia to see the Barrier Reef. But that burst of energy could only last so long and take her so far. Having to stop in the middle of the Sydney concourse to vomit showed us that.

She didn't want to go home, but we couldn't go on any more adventures. She had returned to the couch, not moving most days, and both of us had to accept the inevitable. It was then that Cheryl decided she wanted to die in Venice.

So now we're here, in this little apartment, in this gray city with its dark canals, waiting for Death and his Beast to come knocking on the door.

Chapter 3

One thing about Venice is how tiny everything is. Even things that are meant to be big and impressive like the Basilica or the bell tower in front of it or, well, anything in St. Mark's Square, are small, 'specially to an American. Fortunately, not far from our tiny rooftop apartment, down a tiny alley, was a tiny bar with a tiny Australian in it. After years of making questionable decisions about driving after sinking one too many, it was good to have a bar within walking distance with a friendly face behind it.

I felt guilty every time I stepped out while Cheryl was asleep, but a man can only be alone for so long and Cheryl's condition left me alone most of the time. While taking a short walk one evening I had found the "il Mondiale di Calcio." Something else you have to know about Venice is that after all of the daytrippers get back on their cruise ships and night comes down, the place is dark and empty like there isn't a soul around. But when I stumbled on the Mondiale there was noise and light spilling out from it. Inside was an equal contradiction to the gray stone of Venice. With its polished brass fixtures and wooden walls, it looked warm and dry instead of cold and wet. A crowd was gathered around the only decently sized TV I had seen in ages, cheering for I don't know which team as a two-colored mass of players battled it out on the screen. Unlike Venice or the small apartment I rented in it, the Mondiale felt alive. So I pulled up a chair and ordered a beer.

That's how I met Dennis. I liked him right away. He was an Australian ex-pat tending bar in Italy for reasons of his own and I had just come from Australia to a place where I couldn't speak the language. He liked football which, despite the fact that I always called it soccer just to annoy him, I enjoyed. But I had never really had anyone to talk about it with – in the Marines admitting that you liked soccer was like admitting you were half a fag. And Dennis was more than willing to educate me.

I liked him because any time that anyone asked him how he was (which I did when he handed me the first beer I ordered) he always replied, "It's got its moments." He said it with a thin smile and a flash in his eyes that could have been merriment, but wasn't. No, it was too hard and too cold to be that, but it was a joke – an inside one he thought too cruel or too heartless to be funny to anyone else. I always thought that if he did share, I'd get it, and we'd have a good laugh at ourselves and the world. But I never asked.

Dennis had my usual Urquell resting for me on the bar before I had finished walking in. I had to crouch slightly to get through the door, causing me to think about a tall blonde, not for the last time that day. I sat down, putting my elbows on the bar at either side of the bottle. "How's it?" I asked.

"It's got its moments," came the eternal answer.

I took a drink of the beer, looking at the TV to see who was playing and thinking that summer was over and I should think about switching brews. Something darker.

"How're you?"

I blinked in surprise at the question and it took me a moment to realize that Dennis had asked it. Another thing I liked about him was he was a military man, reserved by nature and training, so I didn't have to worry about having a conversation unless I wanted to start one. In the few weeks I had been in Venice this marked the first time that Dennis had asked me a question without some kind of invitation. In the 'talk first, answer questions later' culture of Italy, I had wondered how he had managed to survive, much less run a successful saloon.

I paused with the beer halfway down to the bar from my lips. "I'm good." A polite lie, but the best I could manage on being surprised.

"Good." Dennis bowed and dipped behind the bar, talking without looking at me, glancing every few moments at the television as he washed glasses out in the stainless steel sink. After a minute or so I went back to my beer, thinking that this freak blip of preemptive conversation was a fluke. Then, "Appreciate your help with the paralytics the other night."

He seemed to be timing his sentences to catch me between drinks, but in this case I didn't mind. Dennis could have handled the three drunk Russians by himself, but when people deal with someone as diminutive as Dennis they frequently underestimate him, particularly if they're drunk. And when people underestimate people like Dennis, people get hurt. I was happy to pitch in. Actually doing something rather than just standing around watching was ... well, it was fun. And a relief. The adrenaline crash that comes after a fight gave us both the chuckles as we watched the Russians hobble away and it had given us an excuse to talk. We had learned a little about each other and liked what we had learned and now I had a person to talk to at my new favorite bar.

"No problem. Any time." I finished bringing the beer to my lips and Dennis stood up in front of me, putting gnarled hands palm down on the bar, looking directly at me for the first time that evening. "So what are you lookin' to grizzle about?"

I stopped and cocked my head at him, not real

sure what he was asking. "What?"

"First time you come in 'ere I could tell you were carrying somethin' with you, but you looked like you just wanted a stool to sit on. Today's the first time you come in here to bend yer elbow and didn't finish off one of those bottles in less than five."

From this sage observation he concluded, "You look like a man who's got something on his mind."

There comes a time in every relationship when a man is asked a direct question by another man and he has the simple choice of being honest or brushing it off. That decision often dictates how the rest of the relationship will go. I thought about it a moment and went somewhere down the middle. Like I said, I was lonely.

"You mean more on my mind," I answered, emphasizing 'more'.

"Ah, well then," Dennis said, mock widening his eyes and dragging out the first vowel, "you'll need one of these." He disappeared behind the bar again and came up with a dark, cleanskin bottle in one hand and two whiskey glasses in the other. He poured a brown liquid into both glasses without asking my permission or forgiveness. He took his own and held it up, "Cheers."

He slung the glass to his mouth and I followed suit. My mouth went numb in a way that wasn't entirely unpleasant and I coughed. Dennis, still holding up his glass, winked at it, then set it down on the bartop and asked, "So what's her name?"

I stifled a second cough, the liquor shorting out a few unnamable parts of my brain. I replied, "I ... I can't remember."

The widening of Dennis' eyes wasn't mockery this time, "Oh then you do got it bad."

I set the glass on the bar and shivered a bit as I

shrugged my shoulders defensively, speaking without thinking. "No it's not like that. She spent most of the time talking to my wife."

Dennis crossed his arms and leaned back against the rear shelf of the bar, eyes not just wide, but openly marveling at me now. "Oh, you mug, you are in a lot of trouble."

"No, God damn it," I shook what was left of the numbness out of my head, "I mean it's not like that. She's just a neighbor. She lives downstairs from the place I'm renting."

Pursing his lips and narrowing his eyes, Dennis nodded as if he were weighing what I was saying. "Well, then, tell me about this neighbor."

"Sophie," I paused a moment to drown the aftertaste of the liquor out of my mouth with my beer. "Her name is Sophie."

"This Sophie seems to have flustered you quite a bit."

"Look," I said, forcing my eyes from the TV to Dennis', "I locked myself out of my place this morning and she let me into the building. For whatever reason, I don't know why because she doesn't speak a word of English, she followed me to the apartment and when my wife answered the door, they met. That's it." I rushed through those words and then returned to the TV, quietly hoping the conversation would move on to soccer. The current topic was making me very uncomfortable for reasons I didn't want to admit to myself, let alone Dennis.

"So you got a wife?"

"Yeah."

"And a neighbor."

"Yeah."

"So when I asked you what her name was, why'd you start talking about the neighbor?"

I squinted at Dennis, feeling like the Mondiale wasn't such a friendly bar anymore and gave him a very solid, "Fuck you."

To his credit, Dennis just chuckled and bounced his hips off the rear shelf. "Alright mate, I'll quit bustin' your balls," he said and went back to washing glasses.

After a moment he asked, "So what's this neighbor look like?"

"Tall. Way tall. Blonde." I bit off each of the words, not wanting to mention the damn near flawless skin or green eyes or the fact that Dennis had said he'd drop the subject not more than a second ago.

Dennis' frame stiffened, then he went back to the sink. "You're over by the San Marco Osteria, yeah?"

"Yeah," I replied, thinking the conversation was finally wandering away from my neighbor. Although his thin build didn't show it, next to drinking Dennis' favorite activity was eating – he always used the restaurants he liked as landmarks whenever giving directions.

Dennis went back to washing and I went back to watching the game.

"And your neighbor is a tall blonde," he stood up to fully extend his arm and held it above his head with the hand bent horizontally, "about this high?"

I took my eyes away from the television and began to glance around without making any sudden movements. It felt like I was searching for an ambush. After a moment I replied with a long, "Yeah?"

Dennis made as if to say something, then shrugged, never leaving his work. "Nothin'."

I gave him an angry shrug and went back to my Urquell. After a few Dennis stood up from the sink and stretched out his back in a motion that's familiar to old men everywhere. He turned to a boy that he paid to watch the bar and said a few words in a language that wasn't Italian. The boy was dark skinned and, I guessed, came from North Africa or Turkey. I supposed Dennis spoke more than two languages. After issuing his command he disappeared into the back.

One thing about the Mondiale, like much of Venice, while it may not have appeared big on the outside often the insides were dark and labyrinthine. For all I knew he had tunnels all the way to the French catacombs in the back.

I was just starting to relax and get into the game when I heard Dennis call my name. I yelled back, "What?"

"Come 'ere for a minute!" was the immediate response. My reaction was irate. I wanted just a few minutes to enjoy my beer and watch a game before I had to head back to Cheryl. But after a loud exchange that began to annoy the other customers he said, "I need help with something, you ingrate."

I let out a sigh, set down my beer, and walked into the darkness of the Mondiale's back. I couldn't see much in the backroom. There was a light that I followed that led into a small storage closet, the light coming from a single bulb hanging from the ceiling by a thin cord. Dennis was waiting for me, facing the door I came in by, with an unreadable but grim expression on his face.

Before I had a chance to ask him what he wanted he said, "Your neighbor, you said she's named Sophie?"

I controlled the urge to let my eyes pan the room again, even though no one but me and Dennis could fit into this closet. I followed it with another long, "Yeah?"

Dennis shook his head emphatically and grabbed

One Sore Rib

a box of booze, handing it to me. "You don't want to have anything to do with her."

I felt my head tilt to the side and the corner of my mouth curl up derisively. "Why not?"

"She's bad news, mate. Belongs to old Don Verdicchio." He went about grabbing another box and laying it on top of the one I already had. Whatever was in those boxes was heavy and my knees bent under the weight.

"Belongs to? What the fuck does that mean?" The idea struck me as stupid and silly and weird in a place that had abolished slavery long before the freedom loving country I came from. I couldn't take it seriously. "And who's this Don guy?"

"Not Don as in Donald, you dill. Don, like Don Corleone."

"You mean Mafia?"

Dennis looked up from the next box he had his hands on and blinked at me in a way that made me feel stupid as only a drill sergeant can. It simply said, "I am telling you the God's truth – why do you doubt me boy?"

"You're serious?" I asked, apparently wanting to prove the credentials of my stupidity beyond question. I knew Dennis wouldn't fun me on something like this but the idea of a kingpin in *La Serenissima* was beyond odd to me. I hadn't seen so much as a weed dealer on the floating isle.

Dennis put the stare on me while stacking another crate on my arms. "Yeah."

I leaned around the pile of crates he had on me and, despite our closed surroundings, spoke in a low conspiratorial whisper, "What's he into?"

"Whatever bad stuff makes the man money." That same phrase could have been used to describe any number of American entrepreneurs, but coming from Dennis in his back room, it sounded sinister.

"That a fact?" I groaned as he set one last box on me, and stepped backwards when he tried to set another, letting him know I was done with this errand. And also to hide the look on my face.

"It is." He carried the last case of beer behind me. "So now you know. Stay away."

"Alright." I said, but my mind was already at work.

Chapter 4

Anyone that's suffered from a chronic illness can tell you, there are two things you worry about in that situation: The first is your own mortality; the second is money. Watching Cheryl disappear into her illness was bad enough. Other than driving to doctor's appointments and making sure my perpetually late wife was punctual and remembered her medication, all I could do was stand on the sidelines with clenched fists. But the money made everything worse.

We had blown through my enlistment bonus with the first round of surgeries. I watched guilt and disappointment mingle in Cheryl's face as we saw the best shot we had at owning a home fold itself into a blur of white gowns, green-masked professionals, machines, scalpels, and treatments. After that, the bills started piling up in numbers I had never seen the like of before – $5,000, $7,500, $12,000.

That's how I found myself up way too late one night, sitting in a second-hand leather chair, sweating over a whiskey bottle with something besides the liquor burning a hole in my chest. I couldn't think and the situation seemed to form walls around me that were impossible to scale. I squeezed the bottle, willing it to burst in my hand, and when that didn't work I sent the electric impulse down my arm to hurl it against the wall, smash it, destroy it. But then my wife's hand, cool and soft, rested on my shoulder and I blinked before my shoulder cocked back to start the throw.

"What are you doing up so late?" Concern and worry showed through her fatigue. The chemo had caused most of her hair to fall out by then and she had

One Sore Rib

asked me to finish it off by shaving her head that afternoon. She had cried the entire time, then cried herself to sleep. The cancer had taken her breasts, her ovaries, and that day, finally, inevitably, her hair, that last remnant of her womanhood. And she was as beautiful to me as she ever was or ever could be, because after a day like that, she had pulled herself out of bed, worried about me.

I looked up at her and blinked rapidly – sweat was stinging my eyes. "Nothing. Just having a drink."

She somehow clucked without making a noise, her eyes softened and her head tilted and I knew she knew I was lying to her. It wasn't something I was very good at. I broke eye contact by wiping the sweat out of my eyes, "I'm just worried."

She placed her hand gently under my chin and brought my face up to look at her. With all of the convictions her ill frame could muster she said, "We will get through this."

I smiled weakly and tried to lie to her again. "I know."

She examined my face with compassion in her own, trying to determine if I was being honest or not, whether she could go back to bed or needed to provide me with comfort. That's when I saw that expression from before, when I wrote the last check that the enlistment bonus would cover, and recognized it again: Guilt. Cheryl, sick and dying, felt guilt for having brought the Beast and his Master into our home.

I blinked, the realization rattling in my head. I shook it out and lied, this time with conviction, giving her a strong smile and brighter eyes. "I'm OK. Go back to sleep."

After a moment she chose to believe me. Bending down to kiss me, we said our 'I love you's and she floated back to bed. And for one moment I thought I could see a dark, four-legged creature following behind her.

So you really can't blame me for doing something stupid. The last $5000 wasn't enough to carry even the smallest of our bills, so I went out and bet those last five on the UT vs. LSU game. I put my money on the Vols since, in the words of a good friend, it was their game to lose.

Fucking Vols. They led the entire game, even up into the fourth quarter, where they were ahead by four points, enough to make the spread. Then they got penalized for having too many men on the field, which gave LSU one more untimed down and a chance to win the game. Which they did.

How does that happen, I ask you? How does a damn near professional team go wandering onto the field with too many men? Aren't knowing the rules part of that job?

It didn't matter. I had very few options. I could give up the cash and try to figure something else out. I could re-up, but Cheryl might die while I was out of country. I could get some shit job that would never pay enough.

Those midnight walls felt even taller and closer and I couldn't stop kicking myself long enough to think straight. So I did the only thing I could think of.

I sat down and wrote out a $5000 check to the biggest bill holder we had. Then I put a stamp on it, kissed Cheryl goodbye, and dropped it in the mail as I went out to find my friend who had given me such sage advice as to bet on UT. I asked him who was holding my chit and, after a little persuading, he told me.

His name was Clarence Castardi (or just CC) and I could find him in the basement of a club called

One Sore Rib

Shotgun Rum. So, like Cortez after he had burned his ships, I went.

The Shotgun Rum was a brick of a building out past Broadway that had all sorts of respectable people in and around it, but it was the sidewalk I was interested in. You ever go down through those doors that lead down into sidewalks? I wouldn't recommend it. The ones on the east side of Rum's were sloped, steel cellar doors that opened to a staircase lined with splintered wood. Following that took me to a single room with a freezer in the back. And in front of that freezer was a desk, behind which, flanked by some men trying their best to look mean, sat Clarence Castardi.

He was a mountain of a man, more muscle than fat, whose bald head came to a bullet point. His mouth hung open slightly as he looked me up and down. One of his men leaned forward and in a few whispered words told his boss why I had come. CC's face continued to hang in its natural expression, which was not a happy one.

"You here to pay your chit?" He flicked expressionless eyes up at me where I stood, tossing some nuts from a bowl on his desk into his mouth. I wasn't offered a chair and I didn't ask for one.

"No," I stated flatly. "I'm here to tell you I don't have it."

"Then go get it. The vig is six over five for every six past, starting Thursday." He spit out the shell of one of the nuts and it arched through the air with the same carelessness as his tone.

I found myself standing at attention, as if I were prepared for a dressing down. "You don't understand – I don't have it."

"Then go get it."

"I don't have it."

He leaned forward, putting his elbows on the desk, rolling his shoulders, the skin around his ears and eyes flushing a bit, and said simply, "Then you shouldn't have bet it." For the first time since I had set out on this mission, sensing Castardi's rising anger, I felt that this might be a very bad idea.

I blinked, then broke my stance to lock eyes with him saying, "I don't have it, I'm not gonna have it, it's not gonna happen." I blinked again and went back to standing at attention.

Castardi pushed himself back off his elbows, causing the desk to rumble forward in a calculated move to intimidate. I'd be lying if I said it didn't work a little. But I didn't flinch and I didn't move and I sure as Hell didn't run.

When I didn't, the big man took a short eternity to examine at me again, this time with eyes that had an expression in them I couldn't quite describe. He scrutinized me like he was trying to figure out if he had found a piece of shit or a diamond.

Abruptly, he asked, "You out of Fort Carson?"

"Pendleton," I replied without thinking. "My wife and I moved out here after I was discharged."

He shifted his weight causing the chair to creak heavily. "Marines," he rolled the word around in his mouth like he was tasting it, not sure if he should spit it out, "always the first boots on the ground."

"Oorah," I said without enthusiasm. The word felt cold and empty down in that basement.

Castardi laid back in his chair, causing some unknown, unoiled part to squeak for mercy. It sounded like a mouse farting.

"You got some stones," he said, nodding. "I'll give you that – to come to my place and tell me that you don't have the money and you're not even gonna try to pay it."

One Sore Rib

I stared back at him, this time feeling shame burning my cheeks. "It's not like that."

"Oh I don't care, Marine." He reached forward to grab another handful of nuts from the bowl and tossed a few into his mouth. Speaking around those bits as he crushed them, he said, "You know as well as I know, though, someone's got to pay. The question is, who's it gonna be?"

I stood there feeling a glimmer of hope, like the sun poking out from behind an eclipse. But I was still in the dark of the moon. With uncertainty and trepidation mixing in me, I stood there.

After a moment Castardi said, "Tell you what, there's a guy out east on Colfax, owes me more money than you. You get him to bring that in, we'll forget all about yours." He shrugged, whatever brief moment of admiration for me that showed on his face being washed away with the universal contempt shared by all pimps and pushers. "This time."

By speaking those sentences Castardi defused the tension in the room causing the two men flanking him to visibly relax. It felt like someone had let all the air back in and I realized I was shaking. Not wanting to show that, I just nodded.

Castardi brushed salt off his hands in broad clapping motions, then leaned forward to scribble on a little yellow pad. He ripped off the top sheet with a flourish of his wrist and handed it to the man on his right, a guy who bore a striking resemblance to Charles Manson, if Manson had been six feet tall. Charlie stepped forward to hand me the sheet and spoke in a surprisingly quiet voice, void of bluster. "That's his name and where you can find him."

I read the sheet, its contents written out in perfectly legible block letters that read EDWARD SEXTON and gave an address. I memorized the address and handed the sheet of paper back to Charlie. This seemed to please Castardi.

I got into my car and called Cheryl to tell her I'd be late. I deflected questions, weakly telling her that an old friend had come into town and we were going to go for drinks. She was clearly suspicious, but chose to believe me. Then I headed out to the east side of Colfax.

The address led to a complex of rundown apartments, built God knows how many years ago in an area that had seen better days. The main selling point of the place was probably the cheap rent. It certainly wasn't the amenities.

I found the apartment, which had a window facing the parking lot, and the darkness inside that told me he was either out or asleep. I hoped he was out, 'cause it would make this easy. If he was in and asleep, he could have people in there with him, maybe a wife or kids, and that would make things hard. So I sat in my car, watching whenever people parked and walked in the door of the building, waiting to see if the light in that apartment window went on.

After a couple hours, a skinny white dude pulled up in a car that said, 'My wife got the house,' and I knew I had found my boy. He took a drunken lope up to the front door of the apartment building and, sure enough, a few moments later the window I had been watching lit up.

I never thought anything that I had learned in Fallujah would be useful in civilian life. As I walked into the central corridor of the building to find Sexton's apartment, though, I could feel that familiar rush of adrenaline going through me. I knocked hard on the door just as I had a hundred times before and stood aside so anyone looking through the peephole wouldn't see me.

One Sore Rib

Despite the blood pounding in my ears I could hear footsteps come towards the door and then the tentative call of, "Who's there?" I wheeled around to face the door and put all my weight behind my foot to slam it in.

It sent a painful shiver up my leg and into my lower back as the door gave way, sending Sexton back away from it, landing him on his ass onto some carpet that was ugly enough to have been there since the '80s. Words started coming out of his mouth in phrases that meant nothing to me. I stepped through the entry, slamming pieces of wood out of my way as I pushed through.

I grabbed him by the collar as he made noises that could have been pleas or excuses while he scratched at my arms. I picked him up and slammed my fist into his face and kept pummeling him until he stopped struggling, but stopped before he quit begging. After a few moments that seemed like eternity, I hoisted him off the ground and pinned him to the nearest wall, my fist cocked back to start laying into him again. By then his words started making more sense against the blood in my ears, cajoling and pleading at various turns, from one sentence to the next. When his legs gave way and he started to slide down the wall I had him pinned to, I picked him up and hit him again.

His nose was pouring out blood by then and he was feverishly looking at me, blubbering through sweat and tears, "It's not my fault, man! I din't do nothin'! Idin'tdonothin'!"

I slammed him into the wall again, locked my eyes onto his and told him: "I don't care."

That's how I ended up driving back to the Shotgun Rum with a grand of Sexton's money in my pocket. I probably should have cleaned up first or gone home to see Cheryl, but I wanted to let Castardi know I could handle myself. He was exactly as I had left him a few hours before, leaning back in his chair and eating nuts out of that bowl. This time he had his feet up on the desk and as I walked back into the room his eyes tracked up towards me betraying more than a little surprise.

"Change your mind?" he asked, going to what was probably, in his world, the most likely outcome.

Without introduction or explanation I dropped the cash roll on his desk and said, "You'll have the rest in three days, plus the three extra points." I wasn't standing at attention anymore – I was tired and my fists hurt and I wasn't feeling too good about what I'd just done.

He pulled his feet off the desk and pivoted in the chair towards me. "That was fast."

"Didn't see a point in wasting time."

Castardi gave me a suspicious eye and eyed my bruised fists. I hadn't bothered washing all of the blood off – there was still a faint layer. "How do you know he'll pay?"

I looked at him, feeling like I was the intimidating one now. "I put the fear of God in him. Nothing scares a man so much as being hit without knowing why he's being hit. Now he knows why I was hitting him and he'll pay just about anything to make sure it doesn't happen again."

Castardi took a moment to probe for a piece of nut from between his canine and incisor as he contemplated that bit of nonsense. When he fished the offending bit out he smiled, but I couldn't tell if he was smiling at me or just from the satisfaction of having gotten rid of an annoyance. "Well, then, in three days time, if he pays up, you're a free man."

The bullet head came up as he leaned forward on

his desk, Mr. Intimidation again. "And if he doesn't pay you'll be three more days down on your debt."

I resisted the urge to blink fatigue out of my eyes and stared down at Castardi with the confidence I felt. "He'll pay," I said, knowing Sexton would.

"Good." With that one syllable Castardi swiveled in his chair again and his feet went back up on his desk. I was dismissed.

I left and went home to Cheryl and our place. Three days later Castardi called me up and offered me a job.

Working for Castardi was how I kept the bill collectors at bay and how I saved up for the trips we decided to take at the end. It wasn't pleasant or good work, but it gave me something to do and something to hit when I needed something to do and something to hit, and that might have saved my soul. Or at least my mind.

Of course, Castardi may have provided me with an opportunity but that didn't change the fact that he was a bastard and not the type of guy to pay sick leave. So when we did decide to take those trips we were working with what I had managed to save and nothing else. By the time we had decided to leave Sydney for Venice I was almost out of cash.

This became painfully clear to me going through security. I was waiting in line with the rest of the sheep, holding up Cheryl when she wasn't leaning on her crutches, watching bags go in and out of the X-ray machine when I noticed mine get pulled off the conveyor belt. I groaned internally as I realized I had left my KA-BAR in it.

I kissed Cheryl on the forehead and stepped through the metal detector, walking to a security guard who was gesturing me over to him while holding my duffle bag. Setting the bag on a table and unsnapping the bindings he asked, "Do you have anything sharp or dangerous in your bag, sir?"

I shrugged and for some smart-ass reason replied, "Probably."

The security guard was not amused and immediately began rummaging through the bag with gusto. A few seconds later he found and pulled out the knife, telegraphing his exasperation with a tilt of his head.

"You can't take this with you in a carry-on bag, sir," his tone held equal parts threat and boredom.

I started to fumble words, put in a bind between my desire to keep the knife and my need to make the plane. As I did, the security guard's expression grew darker and more pinched, clearly tired of idiots like me making his job tougher and then making excuses about it.

What sounded like aluminum chairs from an old school crashing to a linoleum floor caught our attention. I found myself bounding back through the security line to pick Cheryl up from where she had fallen in a clatter of her metal crutches. There were several more minutes of confusion as Cheryl blearily apologized. I tried to explain to the now crowd of security personnel that we didn't need to go to a hospital, that the hospital was no good, and what we needed was to get on that plane and get to Venice.

When the confusion had subsided and the guards' questions sufficiently answered panic and anger gave way to sympathy and Cheryl and I were allowed to pass. As I walked with her to an electric cart that had pulled up for us, the security guard stopped me to give me back my bag.

"You can't take this with you," he said, still holding onto my KA-BAR. His hostility had been replaced by the all to familiar look of pity that I had

One Sore Rib

come to hate.

"I know," I nodded and shouldered my bag.

"Look, mate, I know what this thing is." His expression was one of someone trying to reach out to a stranger, of someone trying to make a connection.

"Then you know what it means to me," I said with an unexplained hostility in my manner. That unbidden emotion caused my left brain to tell me I was acting like an unhappy child who was having a favorite toy taken away.

"Sure, I saw your ID. But I can't let you on board with it."

"Then what good are you to me?" I said in a rush of anger that I instantly regretted.

He blinked at me then, his own anger and something else warring in his eyes. That resolved into, "I can post it to you. Give me the address of your destination."

At this unexpected gesture of generosity I felt my chest go tight and my throat try to lock up. I couldn't speak for a moment but when I could I choked out, "Yeah, that'd be great."

I unbuckled my pack again and rummaged through it until I found the address of the place we'd be staying in Venice. He took down the address and gave me his best guess on how much it'd be to mail the knife.

That's when I realized I didn't even have the cash on me for the postage. He told me he'd post it anyway.

Chapter 5

The next time I saw Sophie it was in a different light. Instead of seeing her as a beautiful woman I saw her as an opportunity. It helped a little.

If I leaned over the edge of the rooftop garden I could see down into the alley to the building's main entrance. The day after my talk with Dennis it was, thankfully, a little sunny. So I picked Cheryl up and walked her to the roof so she could sit on the deck. In her moments of consciousness she gazed out over the sprawling rooftops of Venice and gave them a fragile smile.

A chill wind was blowing off the ocean so I had her wrapped up in her favorite blanket, a ratty purple thing that she refused to part with no matter how many holes it sprang. I topped this off with a knit cap that my sister had made for me before her husband had killed her. I held Cheryl then and talked about the history of Venice I had been reading up on, which lulled her to sleep every few minutes. When she wasn't awake I leaned out to watch the alley waiting to see if I could spot Sophie come or go. Sometime around lunch I saw her blonde head walk out and not long after she came back carrying what appeared to be a grocery bag.

"What are you staring at?" Cheryl asked from behind me.

I nearly jumped with guilt at her voice. Instead I just looked over my shoulder at her and said, "I think I just saw that woman who helped us out the other day come in."

Cheryl nodded without replying so I asked, "You two seemed to get on. Did you want me to invite her up?"

Cheryl gave me a weak, wispy smile with a, "That'd be nice."

I carried her back down to the apartment, laid her on the couch and then bounded down the stairs hoping to catch Sophie before she got to her door.

My feet echoed loudly through the stone stairwell and I found Sophie hurrying with her keys to get inside her apartment. Before I approached she got the door unlocked and swung her body through, keeping a crack open to look cautiously back. We stood there, her glaring at me in the gray light of the stairwell, trying to figure out who I was.

Her timidity struck me as odd after the warm welcome she had given me as a stranger just the day before, but before I puzzled on that anymore she recognized me. She threw the door open completely and greeted me with the warm smile and a "Salve." I couldn't help but notice the nearly flawless skin exposed by the white sleeveless shirt she was wearing, only marred by an ugly black bruise on her upper left forearm.

I grinned like a schoolboy and made gestures, still not trusting the little Italian I knew to convey why I was there. After some rudimentary charades of greeting, I moved on to making chewing motions with my jaw and pointed upstairs, hoping she wouldn't misinterpret it as some kind of invitation to come up and be cannibalized. But her smile just grew a notch and she disappeared back inside momentarily. She came back out carrying what I assumed was the same sack as from before.

I led the way and she followed speaking in singsong Italian that made the staircase a less drab place to be. When we got in Cheryl was sleeping again and Sophie made her way into the tiny kitchen. She set the bag on the center island table and immediately began pulling groceries out of it, laying them out on its butcher-block surface. I thought about trying to tell her that she was the guest and that she didn't need to be cooking, but then worried I'd bungle it and appear ungrateful. After a few minutes of being unsure what to do, I stepped the four feet back into the living room to check on Cheryl.

She was awake then. After her eyes focused, they shifted towards the kitchen. Hearing Sophie's Italian she said simply, "She's here."

Sitting down on the edge of the couch next to her I started to say something, but Sophie popped out of the kitchen and smiled. I think a part of me started to love her then, just because of that smile. It was genuine and even though I couldn't understand what she was saying, it was clear she was happy to see Cheryl.

Most people had stopped being glad to see Cheryl a long time ago. Sure, some came to see her. And yes, they smiled, but it was the timid, reluctant smile of people who didn't want to be near her, the smile of obligation, the smile of fear that they might upset a delicate balance. Or worse, one that said they were uncomfortable being around someone that reminded them of their own mortality and the fragility of their existence.

The two of them started to talk in slow Italian, slow enough that even I could understand a word or two and I caught the word "pranzo." After reaching some conclusion that I missed, Sophie stood, smiled, then darted back into the kitchen. Cheryl settled back into her pillow, smiling as she closed her eyes, saying, "She's going to make us lunch."

Not for the first time since the Venetian adventure had begun I sat uselessly, staring at Cheryl. Sophie moved about in the kitchen chopping, opening packages and speaking loudly, like an old relative who comes to your house, commandeers your kitchen, and yells at you from it, making their presence known in every room. It gave a warmth to the place that I was grateful for even though her chatter meant nothing to me.

    Time dilated in that tiny space and for a moment I felt as if I were living in a photograph. But then Sophie popped that self-involved bubble by slicing into the room, carrying a knife and a tray filled with delicious smelling fruits and meats. She laid it down in between Cheryl and me with a professional flourish, then disappeared back into the kitchen. I hadn't eaten since the morning and snatched up a piece of prosciutto like a starving man.

    Politely and gingerly Cheryl reached out and took the tiniest piece of melon between thumb and forefinger and brought it to her lips. Before she got it there, though, the smell of it hit her nose, causing it to crinkle. I could see the nausea push her back onto the couch as she laid the melon back on the plate.

    A now familiar coo came from the kitchen threshold and I looked up to see Sophie staring at us with a mixture of sympathy and disappointment. I attempted to explain that Cheryl hadn't had much of an appetite in awhile. Cheryl, though, seeing Sophie's crushed, expectant expression, spoke something in quick Italian and held her stomach, showing her fluency in the second great Italian language, gesticulation.

    Understanding immediately, Sophie swept down on the offending tray and removed it from the room. My stomach growled instantly as I sheepishly watched it go, chastising myself for my selfish desires. I began to eat my one piece of pork in smaller bites.

When Sophie burst into the room again, as if my hunger had given me some sort of clarity, I could see her energy was somewhat forced, trying to balance out the negative current in the room. With me sitting on the coffee table across from Cheryl on the couch, she perched her fine bottom on one of the chairs catty-corner from us. Putting her elbow on her thigh and her hand on her chin, she leveled a gaze at us like a host might at an audience of children. She spoke to Cheryl as if to ask, "What shall we do now?"

Cheryl gave her one of her best smiles and spoke to Sophie in their cloistered language. Sophie answered affirmatively, causing Cheryl to grin at me with an old familiar mischievousness and say, "You may go."

"What?" My utterly dumbfounded expression only seemed to increase her enjoyment.

"Go on," she repeated, weakly gesturing towards the door in an imitation of some ailing monarch, "scoot."

"But, I can't just..."

"You," Cheryl dropped the mock expression, replacing it with one of concern, "need to get out of here for awhile. If anything happens, Sophie will be here to help me."

"But what if..." I wasn't able to finish the sentence and the words choked in my throat.

She read my mind though and put a hand on my cheek, the touch of mercy. "It'll be fine."

Sophie had moved to the kitchen and was holding up the white receiver to the ground line, some relic from the 20th century. She was miming its use in an exaggerated manner, having deciphered our conversation and offering to call if I was needed.

"I, ah," in trying to understand her I forgot about our language barrier, "I don't have a phone. Our cells don't work over here, the networks..." Then I trailed off as realized that I couldn't explain and turned to Cheryl.

But she just lay there with her eyes closed, gestured towards the door again and said, "I'll be fine for an hour or two."

So that's how I ended up walking down Piscina De Frezzaria alone in the middle of the day. Up to that point I hadn't gone out onto the island much except at night, but once I got out passed the Hard Rock Cafe, I realized why the locals hated the daytrippers so much. Right next to the most annoyingly American restaurant the canals were filled with boats of tourists, ignoring gondoliers who passed the time singing songs that were probably older than my country. The normally small, quiet streets had become filled with God-knows-how-many people all squeezing and pushing and, most of all, rushing, looking at maps or at devices or trying to squeeze in a family picture. No one took time to appreciate the quiet ghosts of this place that said more than all of their blaring and stomping ever could.

While I understood it, it wasn't the reason I disliked these massive crowds of foreigners in a foreign land. I had a much simpler reason – there's not a whole lot worse than being trapped in your own mind when stuck in a crowd. It's a special kind of isolation that would make for a great enhanced interrogation technique if you could patent it.

What had I been thinking? Why had I invited Sophie up? I had had the beginnings of an idea, but now that I reflected on it, it sounded insane. The one person who had shown Cheryl any kindness and I was going to use her to ... what? Kidnap? Extort?

I felt those walls again, high and closing in, and for a moment, in the middle of all those honest people just trying to enjoy a small piece of an Adriatic vacation, I felt I might scream and rend at my clothes like some Jew from the Old Testament.

That'd make for a story for the folks back home. I had to get out of the streets. I considered heading to Dennis', thought better of it, then reversed course and headed in the direction of il Mondiale.

I walked through the wooden, stooped entrance and my Urquell was already waiting for me on the bar. Dennis was behind the counter, busy with something. I had the feeling he was pointedly ignoring me, but I decided that was probably my own paranoia, guilt at having ignored his well-intentioned advice. I took a pull off the bottle and asked, "How's it?"

"It's got its moments," he replied, finishing up whatever he was doing behind the bar. He dried his hands on a towel. "You?"

"Good," I lied. "Might have more than my allotted share of these today." I paused for another drink, "I've got time off for good behavior." I guess I thought luring him into thinking I'd spend more than usual might improve the disapproval I imagined he was leveling at me.

"That a fact? And where's the wife you've told me about?" He picked up a remote and idly flipped the television's channels.

"With a friend." I tried to sound casual.

He turned to me and his expression told me the disapproval wasn't entirely imaginary. "With a friend? Who's that then? Didn't think you knew anyone around 'ere."

"You know ... the girl."

"The blonde you're all doe-eyed over?"

"Hey now," I felt my own guilt rising at the truth in his words and it threatened to become anger. But Dennis raised a palm towards me, stopping me before I got started.

"Fine then, mate. How about a game of darts?"

The sudden change in conversational direction

One Sore Rib

left me a bit stumped, so I just said, "Sure, yeah."

"Great," Dennis said without much enthusiasm. He then spoke to the haji boy, gesturing to the front door. I wondered about leaving someone clearly not of the legal drinking age in charge, but the bar was emptier than usual, occupied with only the three or four sad-looking locals that were always there. Before I could give it much more thought Dennis had stepped out from behind the bar and led me through the backroom door, flicking on a light as he walked through it.

I had never seen the backroom of il Mondiale with the lights on and I had to take a second to blink the retina burns out of my eyes. It was a contrast to the well-lit front with its shiny brass. Even though it was only a few feet away, the back had a claustrophobic feel to it, with no windows and dark corners that the lights didn't reach. The walls were planked wood that made it feel as if we had just stepped into the hull of an old ship and the furniture complemented this with low set, small wooden chairs and tables. Strange wire decorations hung from the ceiling that could be mistaken for rigging out of the corner of the eye.

Dennis opened a small cabinet on the wall and removed a set of darts with each hand. He handed me one, gestured towards the dartboard in the cabinet and said, "Throw for first."

I stepped up, squared myself against the board and threw, lousily. Dennis casually won the first throw, collected the darts and started to work, destroying me at the first game of darts I had played since before boot camp.

After a few lessons in humility in which neither of us spoke, other than some quiet cussing from me, Dennis lined up for another throw. Offhandedly he said, "So you've left your wife with the woman I warned you about associating with?"

I rolled my eyes. I knew there had been some reason Dennis had pulled me into the back – he didn't want to discuss Sophie and her mysterious man in front of the house. "Come on, man. She's nice enough and the two of them seem to be really getting on."

"Of course they're getting on," he said matter-of-factly as he stepped aside to let me make my throw. I couldn't tell if I heard anger in his voice or if it was my guilty conscious getting the better of me again. "Verdicchio doesn't let her out of that box he's got her in – I'd think she'd be desperate for real company."

"So let her have some company," I replied, sinking a dart into the 17.

He pulled on my elbow with a hand that felt like a hook. Even though I was far taller than him and outweighed him, my feet spun towards Dennis without me having much say in it. There wasn't any doubt now that he was angry. I couldn't tell if he was peeved because I had ignored his advice or because he couldn't stand the general stupidity of his own species.

"Why?" A simple, direct question from a simple, direct man. And one I didn't have a good answer for.

"I thought it was a good idea. Like I said, they seemed to be getting along."

"Bullshit."

"What's it matter?"

"What's it matter? I can understand a man's eyes straying a bit, but I'm dead serious when I tell you it's bad news."

"It's not important."

"Not important? Man! How can you say putting your lovely in danger for no good goddamn reason isn't important?"

I turned away from him and sunk another dart

into the board, the needle all the way in, filling the room with a loud, hollow thunk. "Because she's dying."

Dennis moved as if I had physically struck him, his head tilting like a rung bell with a dazed expression in his eyes. I regretted saying it instantly. "Wha?" he managed after a stunned moment.

Regret or not, there wasn't any going back, so I laid it out all on the line for him – the Beast and his Master and how they had chased us here for Cheryl to wait out her final days. I threw my darts at the board as I spoke. The story kept coming out of me so I marched straight over to the board, pulled out the darts, and started again. I just kept staring at the board, which made it a bit easier.

I could feel him watching me the entire time, though. But when the stretching seconds made it clear I was done talking, Dennis didn't jump in to fill the silence or make empty apologies or feign some great heartache for a woman he had never met. Instead, quietly, after a minute only punctuated by the sound of darts sticking into the board, he said, "Well, right then, you drink for free tonight, mate."

I couldn't help but laugh at that, throwing my head back with hearty gusts until they trailed off, my head drooping as the volume abated. When I was nearly done my chin almost touched my chest, letting out little hiccups of chuckles that were honest and pure enough that they almost felt like tears. Dennis joined me with his own uncomfortable laughter and when it had gone on long enough I only said, "Thanks."

We stopped playing darts then and Dennis disappeared and came back with a bottle of wine, set it in between us on one of his little tables and we started to drink in earnest. The dark recesses of il

Mondiale made it easy to forget that it was still early in the day and Dennis had the boy bring us some plates of cheese and salami, and then later on some sardines. For a short time we forgot about the world outside and joked and drank and ate, and when I did think of Cheryl it was to hope that she was enjoying herself as much as I was.

Chapter 6

Sometime well into the third bottle of wine I realized it was getting on towards dinner. My conscious and my worries got the better of me and I excused myself from Dennis, quickly enough that I felt rude about it. He was in better spirits than I had ever seen him in, though, and he just smiled as he walked me out of the bar.

"Sorry about the backroom waltz, mate," he said, then disappeared into the warm light and brass fixtures of il Mondiale.

It had started to rain in Venice, impossible to notice while in the bowels of the bar. The cold, autumn mist caused the narrow streets and bridges to go a slick, deeper gray, matching the sky above. But even the city as a box of gloom couldn't tamp down my mood. I turned up my coat collar, hunched my shoulders and set back towards Saint Mark's. I pushed my way into the crowds of retreating daytrippers, all huddling back towards their cruise ships and, I hoped for them, some sunnier, warmer clime.

Until, that is, I passed by the richly decorated shops of Venice's main causeways and saw shoes worth hundreds and suits worth thousands. These brought the worry of money back into my mind and my hope for the tourists' warmer destination became Basra. I laughed at my own bitterness and wore a smirk back to the apartment.

The stone entryway into the building was only lit by a few small windows and a skylight which let the gray drab of the sky in, giving the old building the stillness and quiet of an empty cathedral. That is, until I heard the angry pounding, fists on wood, interspersed with even angrier yelling. Stopping in the entryway to shake the damp from my coat I heard the sound travel down the stairwell. I groaned a bit, knowing I'd have to walk past whatever angry drunk was arguing with his wife, but my own shroud of inebriation gave me a bit of courage. So I headed up the stairs, still with enough caution to be quiet.

On the second floor a couple of men were at one of the two doors. The same door I had been knocking at earlier. I slowed my pace as I walked across the landing between staircases, trying to get a covert glimpse of them.

The man doing the banging and yelling spewed what could only be profanities at whoever was inside, while the other leaned casually against the wall. He was shorter and stockier than the one beating a tattoo on the door. The cigarette he was smoking burned bright enough in the murk that I could see he was watching me. I thought about stopping to ask what they were doing, but his steady gaze kept me headed upstairs. A foolish side of me told the rest that maybe I had gotten my doors mixed up and perhaps these fine gentlemen wouldn't be there very long.

The noise and the stink eye I got from the smoker had taken the soft edge off my good mood, riling me with sense of unease. But then I went into the apartment and my agitation jumped up to complete defense readiness.

For a moment I thought the entire place was empty. I quietly clicked the door closed behind me and surveyed the room with a minimum of movement. I was torn between not moving and tearing up the entire place to search for Cheryl. Then I heard her say my name. I smiled, laughing at myself for letting the tough boys downstairs set me on edge.

I walked over to the couch, getting close enough

so I could see Cheryl over its back, her head resting on the arm. Next to her, crumpled into the corner between the couch and the wall Sophie had squeezed herself like a child playing hide'n'seek. She flashed me an abashed smile, almost as if they were playing a game. But Cheryl looked worried in a way that I knew and a glance at Sophie showed a real and terrible fear trying its best to hide under the embarrassment. One of Cheryl's hands dangled off the edge of the couch and Sophie held onto it tightly.

"What's going on?" The boozy good mood completely evaporated off from me in a burning that I felt rise behind my eyes, in a place far back in my head that was just out of reach.

Cheryl turned her head to Sophie, but the girl had buried herself too far into the upholstery and wall paneling for her to make eye contact. Concerned confusion shining in her eyes Cheryl simply said, "I don't know."

I stared at Sophie until she made eye contact. This took a few seconds as she shook with every echo of the relentless beat that traveled up the stairwell. When it did happen, I hooked a thumb over my shoulder and asked, "Why are they at your apartment?" Apartment is, fortunately, one of those words that you can just put an 'o' on the end of and you can sound like some asshole from Jersey trying to fake Italian. Of course, none of the other words in the sentence made sense to her, leaving me feeling stupid for asking the question.

Sophie just trembled so I returned to Cheryl, who was increasingly uneasy. Most likely she had nodded off and woke up to this, so she didn't have much of an idea of what was happening. The entire affair was making me angrier than I knew was reasonable and my own irrationality only made it worse.

"So what the fuck should I do?" I asked with an

exaggerated shrug of my shoulders, raising my hands in the air, "Call the cops?"

Directing my anger at Cheryl only confused her further and a pleading came into her eyes. Her face was a mixture of a lot of things: fear, concern, and not least of all bewilderment at having what had started as a pleasant day take an unexpected and thoroughly nasty turn. "I don't know," she repeated.

She focused on me, reaching out to place a gentle hand on top of Sophie's, her eyes appealing for mercy. I felt my anger focus on her, on Sophie, a flash of hatred for her weakness and my own. I felt some horrible, unreasoning animal moving to get outside of me and onto them, to destroy this, all of it, so it could never be rebuilt.

Then another knock came, loud and primitive, followed by a voice that could have been swearing or calling out to God for answers. And I felt the burning in my eyes roll towards it, to answer that call.

"Fuck it," I shrugged out of my coat. I heard Cheryl call after me as I stepped out of the room, but I just closed the door.

At the top of the stairs I stopped and listened again to the pounding, populated by pauses filled with mad Italian yells. For a second that stretched into eternity an internal voice tried to speak to me in a different language. One of logic, it blended Dennis' advice and all the good advice I had ever gotten in my life. It was smooth and soft and tried to calm the hateful burning behind my eyes. So I crushed it into a ball so small that I could barely hear it anymore and went downstairs.

I moved carefully, slowly, and without a sound down the stairwell, hoping to get to the second floor unnoticed. But the cigarette smoker had eyes on me the entire way to the landing. I stood there, not sure what to say, just watching him watch me as his friend banged ceaselessly on the door.

I stood there, not sure why, letting him hammer on the door, letting the drumming push into my head and feed my anger. I was about to open my mouth to say something when the one with the cigarette shook his head at me and gave a long sigh.

I could see now he was older, with close-cropped dark hair that was receding away from his temples, and that his eyes were baggy with fatigue. He didn't give the impression he was particularly put off that I was standing there, just weary, like my presence somehow drained him. Without moving away from the wall he was leaning on he spoke in short, sharp Italian to the other one who snapped away from the door to glare at his companion. He was the younger of the two, taller and lankier. With the sweat darkening his light hair, dripping down his face, he stood there, panting from his yelling. The sweet internal voice told me to be afraid, but I only stood there.

With his eyes still on me, the older man spoke and nodded in my direction. The young one's eyes slid towards me and his panting mouth formed into a leer. He positioned the carriage of his frame so it was straight to mine and stepped away from the door, crossing the short distance to the stairs. His face bloomed into a malicious smile that I recognized from a thousand young boys. He asked, "What you want, tourista?"

I looked down on him from what felt like a very great height. A calm stillness began to fill me and the stairwell now that the drumming had stopped. "You're making a great deal of noise," I said simply. "It's bothering my wife."

He laughed at me and bobbed up and down, making gestures towards me, up the stairs, then back to me. "Chioccia, why don't you be the man of your house? Go upstairs and tell that bitch to shut it." He kept talking in another string of Italian that sounded similar to the bits he had been shouting at the door.

I stepped closer. "She's very ill. She needs her rest."

The close proximity, the insults, and his constant movement must have been the top guns in his arsenal because now that it had only made me move closer he was taken aback. Uncertain, the slightest shine of fear in his eyes, he twisted around to the older man, silently searching for guidance. His compatriot shrugged while taking a drag from his cigarette. He blew out the smoke and waved the cigarette at me, flatly speaking. I could tell it meant something to the younger one as his entire demeanor changed from doubt to savage glee.

He pivoted back to me, his right hand behind him, so I made a grab for that wrist and kept him from bringing the knife into play. The move pulled him closer, so I could smell the cloying smoke on his breath, and the slam into my larger body stunned him, his mouth going from malicious to agape. I used that surprise to hook my leg around his knee and push on his chest with my free hand. That pulled his feet out from under him, sending him down to the floor, his legs pointing into the air.

He scrambled to get up but stopped on his knees when he realized he didn't have the knife anymore. His astonishment was deeply satisfying. I connected to his jaw with a right cross that sent him back to the floor.

The quick, violent action, the pain in my knuckles, and the knife all pushed a coarse dose of adrenaline through me that washed away the stillness. I took a breath that made my chest swell and turned to the other man with heat in my eyes that felt like it should have incinerated him. Raising my hand up to eye level, I opened it, dropping the knife next to the boy, its metal clattering on the marble of the stairwell.

The older man just made a slight cluck while scratching the space in between his ample eyebrows. I waited to see if he would speak, but he only took one last puff and tossed his smoke to the ground, grinding it into the floor with his shoe. Then he went to the descending stairwell without a word or glance in my direction.

The heat in my eyes became a blistering anger at being summarily dismissed. I moved over to him faster than his indifference would allow him to escape and grabbed him by the back of his collar. Stepping on his ankle and pulling up on his shirt, I took him off balance and then slammed him into the bannister, feeling all of the soft flesh grind into bone. When I pulled him back by his collar again, he wasn't ignoring me, his eyes wide and bloodshot, shocked and uncertain. I gave him a kidney punch and all of his weight went out from under him.

"Don't come back," I said in a vicious whisper that I enjoyed too much. Then I tossed him down the stairs and watched him roll. I had to restrain myself from howling after him.

I took a couple of the deep, gulping breaths I had been wanting since I came down the stairs and let the adrenaline recede from me a little bit at a time. I had a familiar sense of detachment that I didn't want to take back upstairs to Cheryl. I watched the puddle of blood that had formed around the boy's head spread out over a few centimeters until I felt that the reality of it all sink into my chest. I blinked the sweat out of my eyes and rubbed my face, then went upstairs.

Cheryl was sitting up on the couch. She had

coaxed Sophie off the floor onto the coffee table where she sat, hunched over, staring directly at the door. Both of them watched me enter, Sophie with a mixture of hope and uncertainty, Cheryl with concern and something that might have been suspicion.

Before either of them could ask me anything I raised my eyebrows and my shoulders, feigning puzzlement. "They're gone," I said simply. A true statement crafted into a lie to make it sound as if they had just up and walked away.

Cheryl spoke to Sophie for a moment ("sono andati") then back to me. "They just left?" I don't know how long she had been awake to hear their pounding, but the glance she gave me said that their sudden, inexplicable departure was too good a break to be likely.

I made my way around the couch, giving a brief smile to Sophie, all the better to break eye contact with Cheryl as I spoke, "They took off when I came down the stairs. I guess they thought I was trouble." I coupled the last statement with a smile that said, "Who me?"

Cheryl smiled back, at the beginning of another sentence, clearly not completely convinced, but Sophie interrupted her with a hand on her shoulder. She asked Cheryl a barrage of questions, all of the answers to which were "Si." With each affirmative answer she became happier and more relieved, the tears of fear being replaced with happy ones that she wiped away. She finished by hugging my wife like they were fellow survivors. I smiled at that, as did Cheryl, looking at me over Sophie's shoulder. She made an exaggerated noise at the pressure of Sophie's hug, who then apologetically laughed, smoothing out Cheryl's blankets and then running a gentle hand along her scalp. She gave me a quick hug as well and then gathered what few things she had and began heading to the door.

Turning towards Cheryl I jerked a thumb to our exiting neighbor, "I'll walk her down."

"Sure thing, hero." Even in her dilapidated state Cheryl could still muster a bit of appreciative sarcasm.

Following Sophie to the door I just smiled and nodded at her. The warmth of her expression pulled on my dead face a little and I couldn't help but genuinely smile as we left.

Sophie went down the stairs with short staccato steps, punctuating the music of her heels with happy Italian. I glided behind her, keeping an eye on the shadows in case either of our intruders had an inadvisable attack of courage and decided to plan something. But no one was there and the stairwell only echoed with the enthusiasm of Sophie's steps and the liveliness of her voice.

Three steps up from the second landing, she came to a dead stop. I had spied down from the third landing and knew that the kid wasn't still there, so I walked up behind her to see why she had paused. She was as rigid as a board, her hands bunching up the things she had been carrying to her chest, eyes nailed to the landing below. Following her gaze, I saw the small puddle of blood that had been left behind, still red and wet.

I stood behind her, not sure what to say. Without a word, she broke her gaze from the blood and marched around it, in what could have passed for perfect regimental step, right to the door, then quickly disappeared inside.

I sat down on the stairs, deflated. Her reaction to the remains of the violence robbed me of what Neanderthal joy I had gotten out of it. And thinking about that led me to think about what Cheryl would

One Sore Rib

think if she found out. What would happen if the men came back? What if their beef was legitimate and they called the police? What if it wasn't and they came back with more men? What if Sophie wasn't the warm, wonderful person she appeared to be? Or what if she was and I couldn't protect her? Was it even my place to do so? And finally, of course, what the hell had I gotten myself into?

Suddenly, Dennis' advice made a lot more sense. After sitting on the steps long enough that I was sure I wasn't going to be sick, I headed back upstairs.

The afternoon's excitement had clearly drained Cheryl – she wasn't sitting up anymore, but lying back, her face looking pale and sunken, her eyes deep set and far away as she watched me sit down. I felt the corners of my mouth turn down as regret at going to il Mondiale replaced everything else. As if I could fix this with a simple question I asked Cheryl, "How are you?"

She gave me a smile, a wicked half-grin, and said bluntly, "I'm dying."

"Oh sure. But besides that?" I replied, quickly and lightly.

She giggled slightly at our forced levity. "Well, the pain pills are working today, so that's something."

I reached out to the table and picked up the prescription bottle, giving it an exploratory shake. "Looks like we need to get you a refill soon." That opened up a new bunch of worries, but then I noticed a small brown box. "What's this?"

"Dunno, it came for you after you went out this morning."

I pulled open the box and looked inside, my hand rummaging around the packaging. Lifting out the KA-BAR, I held it up against the dying afternoon light. I stared at it awhile, unsure what to do with it.

Chapter 7

I spent most of the next day wondering if someone would show up looking for me. Either friends of the two Italianos or, what was probably a lot less likely, the polizia. Oddly, I thought as little of the police as I did of criminals in Venice having seen none of either. But in the morning I woke up worried about both.

I went through my morning routine as usual. The couple of hours of sobriety and the adrenaline rush after I had left the Mondiale had guaranteed I didn't wake up with a hangover. At least that meant I could get Cheryl out of bed, washed and changed, into a new set of bedclothes easier than on some mornings. She was in better spirits than usual too, sharper and more present, which meant she could sense something was wrong. Throughout the morning I just smiled and lied to her, telling her everything was fine (something I had, lately, become disturbingly better at) while the entire time I had a gremlin on my shoulder whispering evil things in my ear. I told myself it was irrational, that I was being paranoid, but I couldn't shake the knowledge that I was in someone's cross hairs.

After I had laid her on the couch I made my way into the kitchen to make myself some coffee. While that was percolating I performed the ritual of brewing Cheryl's medicinal senna tea and pounding some fruit into the sludge that served as her breakfast. She hardly touched it anymore and the exercise filled me with a growing sense of futility, but I couldn't stop doing it. The ritual carried a weight of its own now, one that transferred from it to me. Like a man walking to an inevitable destination I felt each part of it get more difficult as it went on, forcing me to think and dwell on things that I would have rather avoided. But I liked to think in doing it I was helping carry some of Cheryl's burden. That's bullshit, of course. Dying is something you do alone. Sometimes you just do it with witnesses around.

But she needed to eat, or at least try to as much as she could, or the process of dying was going to be even more unpleasant than it already had to be. Eventually, I knew, she'd fall into a sleep and not wake up, cease to eat and drink, then cease to do anything at all.

On this day, though, I brought the tray out with her fruit slurry and tea and she was awake and smiling, laying in the sliver of warm sun that came through the drapes. I set her breakfast down and remembered why it was that I did this everyday. Some days her smiles were only a weak reflection of the woman I once knew, but even on those days it only took a touch of her hand or a peck on the cheek to make me want to keep her around for as long as I could. On the days the smiles were missing the memory of them was still enough to make me want to give her as much comfort as I could while we waited for the Beast to bring his Master.

But today her smile was strong and her eyes bright and I felt the weight in my chest evaporate to whatever dull, gray place it went when it wasn't torturing me.

"Thanks," she said, trying to push herself into a sitting position.

"Well, next time you can get it yourself."

"Har, har," she mimicked a baboon idiot's laugh, jutting out her jaw to complete the teasing.

I gave her a smile that said I was laughing at her, not with her, then, "That's so sexy."

"Please, I haven't been sexy in a long time."

"Hey now, don't talk like that. I'll have to jump your bones just to prove you wrong." I pulled on the hem of her nightdress playfully and gave her a wide smile that only hurt a little.

"Oh, good, then you can take me to the hospital after to get me treatment for the multiple fractures."

It's what passed for humor between us in those days. Like both of us, though, it had become tired and we let the banter die out as Cheryl tried a sip of her drink.

She coughed a bit and I resisted the urge to pull her up into a straighter sitting position or ask her if she was OK. It would just annoy her and neither would do any good. She tried another sip and then gave up. I could tell she wasn't going to drink anymore, but she held onto the cup.

"Where'd you go last night?"

"To the bar."

"To the bar," her tone carried mock surprise and just a hint of disappointment.

I ignored it. "Yep. Dennis and I had a nice, casual lunch while you and Sophie..." I trailed off, having stepped onto the conversational landmine I had spent the entire morning expertly avoiding. Trying to dance my way off it, I quickly asked, "What is it that you two were up to while I was gone?"

"Hot sapphic sex!" was her instant reply, it bursting out of her with all of the fake enthusiasm of a *Penthouse* letter. I laughed out load, louder and longer than I intended, snorting as I did. With her emaciated face and the way she popped her eyes open and snapped her jaws in the answer, it appeared as if she had announced her intention to cannibalize Sophie.

She slapped my knee after my laughter started to trail off, telling me, "It's not that funny, perv."

I wiped the tears out of my eyes, still grinning and apologized. "So what did you really do?"

She shrugged, then adjusted the sheets that she had moved off of herself in doing it. "Just like I said – teaching her a bit of English."

"She does love to talk."

"No kidding. She barely shut up until the banging downstairs started. Then I couldn't get a word out of her."

"So she never told you what that was about?"

"Anne Frank made more noise."

"That's weird." I trailed off, unsure of our neighbor, what to say about her, or if I should have listened to Dennis' advice.

"Yeah. So you didn't get a look at the people making the noise?"

"Nope," was my quick response. I could tell straight away that she didn't believe me and probably hadn't believed me the entire time.

Her eyes narrowed a bit and she shook her head slowly from side to side as she leaned closer to me, "So they just were up and gone when you went downstairs?"

"Yep." Why one persists in folly is not a question to which I have the answer.

"Really?" Cheryl stretched out the R in her question, bringing the rest of the word home quick behind it.

"Well," I struggled to come up with some sort of answer that didn't make me feel more the fool than I already did. "There may have been some," I paused, selecting the next word with care, "urging."

"Urging?" She arched an eyebrow, completing a sardonic mien.

"Encouragement," I said, as if trying to help.

"And by encouragement you mean threats and intimidation."

I shrugged and smiled sheepishly. If I could get

out of this without admitting to actual violence, I was willing to accept it as a plea bargain.

A knock on the door interrupted us. Rather than relief at getting out of my questioning I felt all of the irrational fears that had been haunting me through the morning reach up out of my gut and grab me by the throat. Something of this must have shown on my face because Cheryl asked, with a touch of concern in her voice, "Are you expecting someone?"

"No," I said, pursing my lips and raising my eyebrows, trying to hide my disquiet with perplexity. I got up from the couch, "Maybe it's Sophie here to help you badger me about yesterday."

"Knowing your luck they were just friends of hers she was having a misunderstanding with."

"Right," I said, walking towards the old door. Out of all the options I had imagined Cheryl's suggestion sounded like the best one, if the least likely. "That would make me popular."

"Eh, you never like people anyway," I heard from the couch. She must be in high spirits today, I thought, to be giving me this much grief.

I opened the door and looked out onto the landing and there was Sophie in all of her blonde Italian glory. She was smiling a radiant smile, with her body coyly turned half away from me, her hands grasping the bag straps hanging from her shoulder. She had a wide-brimmed straw sunhat on that had a purple trim that matched her sundress. It reminded me that it was sunny outside that day.

Whatever feigned complexity I had been putting on for Cheryl became real with my pleasure at seeing Sophie. I smiled and stared at her, quietly laughing out, "What're you doin' here?"

She bobbed up and down gaily for a moment then bent at her waist, putting her face towards me, which

One Sore Rib

brought her to a little below my height. She spoke in lilting Italian of which I understood none. But it made me smile wider.

I tried to ask what she was doing, but she just continued to smile and bounced past me into the apartment. I followed, my head cocked like a confused puppy.

Five steps of her long legs took her into the living room where she announced herself to Cheryl who remained on the couch. Not waiting for a response from my wife she continued to chatter and walked past the coffee table, over to the wall opposite the couch, and reached up to grasp the curtains and flung open the drapes, letting the morning light pour in.

Reversing course, Sophie walked briskly to the couch and started pulling blankets from Cheryl. My protective instincts kicked in and whatever fondness I felt for Sophie evaporated. I crossed the room, put myself between Cheryl's weak protests and the other's continued Italian and took Sophie by the wrists.

That was the first time I touched her. It was a hostile gesture and I instantly felt ashamed.

I let all my hurt show on my face and asked Sophie, "What are you doing?"

I felt a calm, soft hand on my shoulder then and heard Cheryl say, "It's alright." I released Sophie's wrists. She was just as surprised and a little hurt, pulling her hands to her, closed.

"Sophie," Cheryl spoke and even though I wasn't looking at her I could tell she was smiling. Her next question was in Italian, but I assume it was something like, "What are you doing?"

Sophie stepped away from the couch, towards the window, all of her hurt forgotten, and exuberantly gestured at the window and the beautiful sunlight pouring through. She got about three sentences into her happy speech when Cheryl started to say, "No," again and again.

I looked over at Cheryl to see her shaking her head and then back at Sophie, who was now gesturing towards herself. My brow furrowed and I stated, "Cheryl's too weak to go outside."

Cheryl must have said as much in Italian because Sophie only smiled wider and gestured for me to follow her as she swished her way back towards the door and into the hall. I followed, suspicion reigning in my gait. By the time I had gotten out onto the stairhead Sophie was standing by the open elevator door. In the tiny box sat a wheelchair that looked brand new, all shiny chrome and black plastic.

I shook my whole torso in confusion, since shaking my head didn't feel like it was enough. I stared at Sophie, about to flatly refuse her. This time, though, as she leaned into the elevator slightly, gesturing with both hands like a game show hostess, I saw more than just the beauty that I wanted to see. I saw the slight apprehension around her eyes, her smile fragile like a china plate.

I shrugged, uncertain of what I'd just come across. "Sure, what the hell." I stepped into the elevator, took the wheelchair by its back handles and pushed it through the still open door of our Venice apartment.

I wheeled it around into Cheryl's view, trying to give the gesture a showman's flourish as I pushed it out, gleaming, into the morning light. I almost added a 'ta-dah' but couldn't quite muster the enthusiasm for it.

Cheryl's eyes fluttered open. Squinting through the light at the wheelchair as if she didn't recognize it she asked, "What's that?"

I could feel Sophie standing behind me, nervous energy barely suppressed, as I answered, "It's a wheelchair. I think your new friend wants to give us a tour."

Cheryl blinked again, setting the cup she had been holding onto the coffee table, "Is that a good idea?"

"That's entirely up to you," I replied in the same level, flat tone a captain of mine had used on me when there was a difficult mission decision to make. "Do you feel up to it?"

I was not always an expert on reading the emotions of my wife, but in this case the ones that went through her were as obvious as someone painting them onto her face with a flashlight. I didn't say anything, just watched and waited for her to make up her mind. Cheryl rolled her head back onto her shoulders and I could see that fatigue was winning. If it hadn't been for Sophie standing behind the wheelchair with an increasingly fragile smile, I think exhaustion would have won. Eventually, though, Cheryl brought her head back up, this time wearing that old devil-may-care grin, and said, "What the Hell."

While I don't know if Sophie understood Cheryl, she clearly understood the sentiment as she clapped happily at my wife's response and jumped a little in the air. And then, with a quickness that I wasn't entirely comfortable with, she started getting ready for the operation to move Cheryl from the couch to the chair.

Moving someone who is gravely ill is never a quick or easy thing. I'd imagine it takes as much preparation as leaving the house with children, but the children are heavier and sometimes less lucid. However, Cheryl was having a good day and it was hard to say how long her energy, as it was, would last, so the blankets came off, the clothes and shoes went on, and I picked her up and moved her to the wheelchair. She was as light as a feather and I tried to ignore that fact for the umpteenth time. I blinked my eyes and caught my breath as Cheryl curled against my chest for warmth.

Sophie stood behind the wheelchair like a diligent nurse. She gave me a sad, sweet smile and simply angled the chair towards the door, making it easier for me to deposit Cheryl in it.

I wheeled out to the elevator only to discover that me and the wheelchair couldn't both fit into it. So I rolled Cheryl in, leaving her facing the rear of the elevator with her back to the door. She craned her head towards me and even though the back of the chair blocked most of her face I could tell she was smiling. "See you at the bottom, yeah?"

I hit the first floor button. "I'll be down there before you are."

I waited until the doors on the elevator closed, prepared to run down the three floors to beat Cheryl to the bottom. At the stairhead, though, stood the forgotten Sophie, smiling as patiently as before. Which was good because I nearly barreled past her. But when I started to brush by she slipped her arm into mine and looked me in the eye as if challenging me to drag her down the stairs because she wasn't letting go.

I smiled at her – and noticed she was wearing flats. She couldn't have been more than an inch or two taller than me and was thin as a wisp, and the way she laid her arm in the cradle of my elbow was just as light, but there was something in her bearing that let me know she was setting the pace. When she could see the recognition of that in my eyes she spun on her heels and led me down the stairs, bopping at the ankles with each step, causing her entire carriage to rise and fall in the most minute way, down each one. I kept turning away from Sophie to watch Cheryl descend in the glass cage of the elevator. We walked like that for a bit until the elegant irreverence she carried herself with made me feel too-serious and foolish as such, so I smiled and resigned myself to being in the company of a beautiful stranger for a short period of time.

Once we were reunited with Cheryl and out the front door, it became painfully clear that Venice was not a city one should see by wheelchair. It was obvious that Sophie knew her way around and was carefully selecting the smoothest of walkways. But no matter how careful we were in our pathfinding or how cautiously we proceeded there was always a sotoportego that was too uneven or a bridge too crowded. I could see Cheryl grimace with every bump from the road or a person. But after the seventh or tenth time I asked her if she wanted to go back to the apartment she stopped trying to patiently reassure me and just told me to shut up.

So I did. As the three of us went along Sophie walked out in front and began to point out the parade of Renaissance wonders we were passing. Cheryl kept her head up and her gaze wandered from Sophie and to the buildings and churches (mostly churches – Venice has a lot of churches) and back again as the other woman spoke, smiling as Sophie pointed out something particularly beautiful or made a joke announced with an airy laugh. I didn't understand a word of it, but watching Sophie walk along the canals in her sundress was enough to keep me entertained. I was, after all, married but not yet dead.

There were fewer bridges to cross on the way from San Marco to Castello so we ended up heading east, eventually breaking into what Sophie told us was the Riva degli Schiavoni, a wide-open promenade that curves itself around the basin on the southern end of the island. For the first time in what felt like a long time I could feel the sun on my face and the breeze coming in off the ocean. Cheryl had lifted her head as if to catch the rays of warmth or the briny smell the wind brought in. She was smiling. I turned to Sophie to thank her with a smile of my own.

But Sophie wasn't looking at us. Cheryl, leaning back in the chair and swaddled in blankets, didn't take much notice of the change, but Sophie had stopped smiling and the irreverent gait she carried herself with had disappeared, replaced with a near skulking pace. The sunhat and big sunglasses did a good job of covering up her face and hiding her expression, but the furrows radiating out from around her eyes were unmistakable.

That's when it occurred to me that maybe the hat and glasses were about more than just keeping the sun off Sophie's fair skin. Leaning on the wheelchair, I started following her gaze into the over-crowded market stalls of the promenade, seeing if there was anyone I might recognize or that was paying a little too much attention to our trio. I felt the old instincts come back, like I should be scanning the crowd for someone fiddling too much with a cellphone or scratching at their chest suspiciously. I never figured I'd be wheeling my wife into a combat zone.

That's when I spotted the Old Man and the Kid. Of course, they weren't – even in the dark of the stairwell he hadn't looked that old and the kid was older than some Marines. But that's how I had come to think of them. They had picked a good place, a white church that had a lot of tourist traffic around it so it appeared like they might just be standing around posing for pictures. But something about the way they held their cigarettes too close to their mouths or brought their heads together to talk set them out from the crowds of tourists that were beautifully, blissfully inconspicuous.

I kissed the top of Cheryl's head and said, "I'm gonna grab a snack."

She smiled at me, happy but stupefied with pain and fatigue. I regretted bringing her again, but I only said, "There was a stall back there selling koulouri. I'm gonna go grab some."

Cheryl nodded a tired consent and I made a quick gesture to Sophie for her to take the wheelchair. She jumped minutely, afraid and unsure of what to do, but I didn't give her a chance to respond and walked back towards the stall. I did so without glancing back at the ladies, with all the determination of someone abandoning them forever.

I stopped in front of a booth with the intent of making a quick purchase, but the fat, brown-skinned Tunisian in the stall started speaking to me the moment he made eye contact on my approach. He spoke and waved his hands ceaselessly over his goods as I picked over them. It was annoying, but I had gotten used to ignoring the flailing, emphatic, insistent, and one-sided haggling of Mediterranean merchants. I let him babble on, pretending to evaluate his wares, his gestures making a perfect cover as I watched Cheryl and Sophie move further and further away.

I gave it what felt like an interminably long time, keeping my head down, glancing up occasionally to watch the situation. Eventually, I spotted the Kid smack the Old Man's arm with the back of his hand, point to me and then to Cheryl and Sophie. I kept my head down, trying to ball my presence into something that was small and inconsequential. Out of the corner of my eye I saw the Old Man flash between me and the girls, smoking his cigarette and weighing his options.

He nodded, then he and the Kid moved off the church's stoop and headed towards the women with the double time step of men trying to move quickly without looking like they were trying to move quickly. I tried to estimate how much time they would need to get to Sophie and planned an interception around it.

I started to move in. The body language of everyone in the two pairs was miles apart. The Kid had the same bouncy, bravado step that he had in the stairwell, while the Old Man held up his hands in a call for reasonableness. Cheryl was fully aware now, glancing at them with uncertainty in between intervals of scanning the crowd for me. Sophie was behind her, the big hat and sunglasses unable to hide her alarm, the weight on her back foot like she might break and run.

I realized I had been running my thumb around the pommel of my KA-BAR that I had hidden in the small of my back, stuck between my pants and coat. I stopped and made sure both of my hands were visible as I came up behind the Kid and Old Man. Cheryl saw me first. The two men must have seen the relief come across her face 'cause they swiveled to face me. The Old Man glared at me with barely concealed anger while the Kid was only just able to cover his fear with a sneer.

The Old Man continued to hold up his hands while staring directly at me, not so foolish as to treat me with the disinterest that he had before. When the Kid's right hand disappeared behind his back, I just gave him a simmering, cautionary eyeball and then glanced at the people around us. The Old Man moved to gently put his hand on the Kid's elbow. Sufficiently certain that neither of us was going to do anything stupid he looked at me as if our meeting were just an honest mistake and said, "Permesso." Then he led the Kid off.

I got behind the wheelchair, nearly pushing Sophie

One Sore Rib

out of the way, and said, "Let's go home."

I leaned into the chair and pushed, spinning it back west. Sophie trailed behind, guilt pushing off of her like some kind of force field. The adrenaline was still simmering in me and with nowhere for it to go I felt a glowering anger towards her growing. It built as we walked along and when it reached a point where I thought I couldn't contain it I prepared to say something to Sophie, sure that my tone and expression would make my message clear. But then Cheryl started to laugh.

I couldn't be anything but happy at first to hear her laugh, but she continued to giggle, pointing up at the mural above the door of another church we were passing. I felt something in my chest shift and the happiness drain away – the laughter wasn't Cheryl's usual loud, disregarding laugh, but the giggle of a sick child.

I walked in front of the wheelchair and crouched down to check on her. She continued to smile, but her face looked phlegmatic and jaundiced. I could feel concern paint my face as I asked, "What's so funny, honey?" trying to put a bit of singsong in my voice to go with the rhyme.

She pointed to the angel in the mural and said quietly, "He's got a fish in his pocket."

I looked up at the mural, feeling confounded as I searched over the angel for a fish. The angel was a stark figure standing against a blank background that had been worn away by centuries close to the sea. Garbed in a smooth white robe, I couldn't see that the messenger had any pockets, and there was no fish to be seen.

I turned back to her, not bothering to hide my concern and got halfway through a sentence explaining there was no fish when I stopped. She pointed and smiled, staring right through me, the smallest bit of drool on her lower lip.

Matthew Cooper McLean

    I picked her up out of the chair and carried her the rest of the way. We didn't bump into hardly anyone on the way back. The callous people of Venice and even the oblivious daytrippers are surprisingly sympathetic when you have a dying woman in your arms. We got back to the apartment and I laid her down on the couch, wrapped her in blankets. I knelt next to her and prayed to the Beast and his Master to take this drooling, withered woman away and give me back my wife, if only for a little while longer.

Chapter 8

Cheryl spent the rest of the day and that night on the couch in a sleep so deep it could have been a coma. She had moments of consciousness, but not ones where she was really there – she spent those staring blankly off into space, her eyelids fluttering, only punctuated by the occasional muttering and the odd, terrifying scream. There might have been a knock at the door sometime during the night that could have been Sophie, but I ignored it and it did not repeat.

I dozed in fits and starts until I felt the morning sun through the living room windows and a cold hand on my own. Cheryl, still on the couch, had her arm pushed out from the cocoon of the blankets I had wrapped her in, her hand on top of mine. I slipped my hand out from under hers and placed it on top to give a gentle squeeze before falling back to sleep.

When I woke up again Cheryl had retracted all of her limbs back under the warm comfort of the blankets, but her face was peeking out at me, her smile telling me that whatever hallucinogenic hemorrhage had taken hold of her had passed. "Hey," she said.

I smiled back, and I could tell that my most winning smile couldn't hide my fatigue and worry. Cheryl looked at me and as my emotional state registered with her I could see the happiness of her smile dim a spell. A piece of me hated the rest because I didn't have the strength to hide it from her.

"Hey," she said again after I didn't respond. She blinked fatigue out of her eyes and then glanced around at the apartment in confusion. "We're back."

"Yep," I tried to keep my own tone neutral, to

filter out of it the deepening concern stirred by the fact that she clearly didn't remember much of yesterday. She rolled over to me, examining me more carefully, then towards the windows. Taking stock of the fresh morning light, adding it to my unshaven, haggard appearance, she quickly deduced, "It's tomorrow," blink, "today."

"Yep," I said and got up from the floor, stretching out what kinks I could.

"What happened?"

I leaned down to kiss her forehead. "We shouldn't have taken you out. It was a little too much."

Cheryl's face screwed up and for a moment I thought she might cry, but whatever emotional well that was spilling out crashed against the dam of her will. Her expression became one of a sustained effort as she tried to claw back details of yesterday. "I remember Sophie showing up and going out in the wheelchair..." she drifted off as I stood up to put my fists into the small of my back and stretch it out.

"And then we had to bring you back," I kept my eyes on the ceiling, filling in her gap with another lie of omission.

She checked herself physically under the blankets like someone who had forgotten their keys, "That's it?" I smiled in lieu of answer, not wanting to embellish on my falsehood. So I got up to make breakfast instead.

As I started towards the kitchen her tiny hand snaked out from under the blankets to hook a forefinger into my belt loop. I stopped, the gesture unwelcome, too raw and exhausted from the night before to let myself feel the affection she was trying to share. I scowled at her, then down at her hand, saying, "I need to make breakfast."

She retreated under the blanket again, a little hurt

at that, but just replied, "Sure."

There's a strange alchemy in trying to hold together your emotional state without letting those around you onto your inner turmoil. Particularly when the person you're hiding it from is the cause. That morning, my secret recipe consisted of orange juice (the European variety that I never cared for as much as the American counterpart) and coffee spiked with a bit of vodka that I had brought back one night. Watching the vodka disappear into the coffee like the rainbow of a gasoline slick diluting in water, I knew it was a bad idea. But I did it anyway.

I crushed up fruit and what was left of Cheryl's pain pills into her morning slurry. Dumping the last two in, I shook the bottle again to verify there were none left. That meant there was only one more bottle – maybe a few days supply.

Her breakfast ready, I went back out into the living room. She was happy as before to see me until she realized what I had in my hand. Her expression curdled as I moved closer with the fruit and she receded back into the cubby of her blankets.

"Eat," I said in a commanding, Neanderthal voice as I shook the cup at her. "You need it."

"Says the man who's drinking his breakfast," she replied with all of the stubbornness of a disobedient child. I couldn't tell if she could smell the vodka or if she was just disapproving of a caffeine breakfast, so I just pressed on with the offering of the cup rather than deal with either possibility.

She took the cup, not willingly or without petulance, but she took it, even if it was pretty clear it was only to please me. The physical exertion of yesterday's trip and the phantasmagoria of last night's dreams must have done wonders for her appetite, though. After a few moments of half-heartedly

One Sore Rib

sucking on the straw her eyes popped a little in surprise and I spent the next several minutes in silence as she happily drank. She rocked her head, appearing to hum a little tune as she did.

I laid back into the couch, gazing out through the window across Venice's slanted rooftops and out to the vast precipice of nothing beyond where the city ends and the sea begins. I wondered why we hadn't bothered opening the curtains earlier. Even with the constant overcast of the sky it had a kind of desolate beauty that was still a better view than the burgundy color of the drapes. It had taken a stranger walking into the house to pull back those curtains to show us that. Thinking on that got me thinking about Sophie and that got me angry.

Eyes still straight out the window I asked, "Do you remember the men you and Sophie ran into?"

Straw still in her mouth, Cheryl rolled her eyes towards the ceiling, giving the question thought. "I remember something about men ... There were two of them?"

"Yeah," I squinted my eyes as a beam of light broke through the clouds. "Who were they?"

Clear-sighted despite the most activity she had in weeks, Cheryl brought her blue eyes down to me and said earnestly, "How would I know?"

I took a deep breath, trying to remember it wasn't Cheryl I was angry at and asked instead, "I mean, what did they say? Did they identify themselves?"

Cheryl pulled her blanket over herself, receding into it a little, and for the first time I realized she was uncertain and a little afraid. "I didn't really understand what they were saying. They weren't talking to me anyway, they were talking to Sophie."

"And you don't remember what about?"

"No," she let the straw that she had been idly

chewing on fall out of her mouth as she asked, "Why?"

Careful to continue not looking at her, staring out across the tiled roofs beyond, I answered, "I think they were the two men that were at her door the other day."

"Oh." Whatever fear that might have shown a second ago disappeared as Cheryl went back to her straw. "Well it's a good thing you were there then."

The casualness with which she made the pronouncement and the childish joy she chased the straw around with her tongue fanned the anger I was trying to keep down. "That's it?"

"What?" She blinked over her cup innocently, intentionally overplaying the expression, making it clear she was being obtuse.

"That doesn't bother you?" I heard the anger in my own voice as I rose to take the bait.

"What doesn't bother me?"

My frustration got the better of me and I blurted out, "She came up here and invited us out, Cheryl. She was using you like a shield, betting that those men wouldn't do anything with us around."

"Do anything? You mean, like, get violent?"

"Yes!"

"Why do you think they'd get violent?"

And just like that, she'd caught me. If my story about the men disappearing the other day had been true, why would I be worried about them being anything other than civil in the crowded, public spaces of Venice?

"I, ah..." There's always at least a moment or two when the fish flops around on the bottom of the boat, where you have to let him realize he's caught. I just sat there, staring out the window with my mouth open.

Cheryl, with the effort and expression of someone climbing out of a hole, pulled herself up on the couch into a sitting position, kneeling forward onto her raised knees, closer to me now. "They didn't just leave the other day because you "urged" them, did they?"

"Well," my brain wiggled one more time, flopping around in my skull as it tried to come up with one more lie to get me out of this. But then it twitched, ceased, and I said, "No."

"So what happened?"

Not seeing a point to saying anything else, I told her about going downstairs, being threatened by the Kid and my fight with him. For a moment I considered leaving out the knife or the rather unnecessary assault on the Old Man, but the truth felt better than the falsehood so I just let it all out.

She paused, the slurry forgotten, leaning back on the sofa and giving this new information some thought. I waited, the moments until her reply dragging out the more I waited. When she finally turned back to me her eyes had a hard determination that robbed the blue in them of their beauty.

"So you think that there are a pair of violent men looking for Sophie?"

"Yes."

"And you think Sophie asked us out the other day because she needed protection?"

"Yes."

"Because these men are looking for her at her home and in public?"

"Yes."

"So she wanted to use us as a shield?"

"Yes."

"So you sent her, alone and unarmed, downstairs, to wait by herself for them?"

I blinked. The conversation had been going in the direction I had expected until that last bit. "What?"

"You idiot." I could tell by Cheryl's condescending

smile that there wasn't any anger in the statement, but I was still befuddled by it. It didn't help when she added, "Go get her."

"What?"

She leaned forward again, some unknown piece of tumor biting into her midsection, causing her to wince with pain. "Go get her. You can't leave her alone down there."

I shook my head. "Cheryl, if she's not going to the police then --"

She interrupted, "Then what?" She gave me a challenge, daring me to go further. And for a second I almost did, telling her that she probably brought this on herself, that she may have stolen from these men, or owed them money, or wronged them in some fashion. If she wasn't going to the police whatever was going on was probably her fault. But Cheryl's stare and the clear and easy way she had cut through my lie to push me to the truth made me wonder how much she might suspect about my work with CC. Did I really want to talk about that? No. So I changed tactics.

"Did you miss the part of the story with the knife? These men are dangerous."

She laughed, a hard, honest guffaw, her head whipping back to belt it out at the ceiling. "What're they going to do, kill me?"

I wasn't sure who she was asking, but then she lowered her head and said, "Go get her."

I stared at her, trying to discern if this was some kind of madness like yesterday's. But Cheryl wasn't the type of woman who wanted a lot of things in her life and our marriage had survived, in part, because I had come to recognize that when she did want something she wanted it hard.

I nodded and got up from the couch. As I headed towards the door she spoke to my back, hidden by the lip of the couch. "You need to stop worrying."

One Sore Rib

I felt something in my chest pinch at what sounded like a futile and hurtful piece of advice. "How'm I supposed to do that?" I asked, an edge in my voice I wished wasn't there but I knew she wouldn't miss.

Her voice carried out from behind the couch again. "It's easy. What's there to worry about? I'm dying. It's a foregone conclusion."

The truth of what she said settled on me like a weight, but it didn't strip me of my anger. It just made me feel unjustified in feeling it. It was immature and juvenile but I took solace from the cold heat of it. Then I put it aside and said, "Those are all true statements. You'll pardon me if I don't find much comfort in them."

With exaggerated grunts and groans Cheryl pulled herself up onto the back of the couch until she had her arms and shoulders over the edge so she could face me. It would have been funny if the sounds had come from a muppet instead of a dying woman. Cheryl examined me for a moment with a bit of that mischievousness in her eyes until she realized I wasn't going to laugh. Then her expression became a tenderness that I only would have believed coming from her.

"I didn't say it was comforting. I didn't say you shouldn't be sad. I just said there's no point in worrying about it."

That pinch from earlier came back and this time it brought friends and I felt my chest threaten to collapse. I opened my mouth to try and say something. Not even the croak I felt in my throat came out. Cheryl watched me struggle for a bit, then smiled, a great calm and beauty around her eyes that had just before been hard, saying, "Go get her."

So I did.

Chapter 9

I don't know if it's Italian women, women in general, or just Sophie, but she started squawking something fierce the moment I started to grab all her clothes. I figured I'd have a moment or two of shocked silence before she began to put up a fight, but no such luck.

Once down the stairs my residual anger caused me to knock on the door louder than I intended to, which made me worried Sophie wouldn't answer. She did answer, but with a timidity I had seen peek out from behind other doors. I felt bad about inflicting that on her so I tried to make up for it with a friendly grin. The smile I got back made me forget about being mad at Sophie and, to be honest, made me forget for a moment that I had a wife. Then I remembered both and pushed my way past her. I heard a playful, "Oof!" from her that let me know I hadn't hurt her.

The apartment wasn't that different than ours, an old interior of dark wood that someone couldn't let go of but still tried to modernize, with everything small, compact, and squeezed into as many corners as possible. I saw that it had a spiral staircase just like ours upstairs and, since the master bedroom was up that in our place, I assumed that's where hers was as well.

I started up the stairs two at a time, getting caught around the tiny axis of the spiral until I felt like a stripper bending around the pole. Sophie realized where I was headed and the playfulness left her voice, her tone becoming indignant. I could hear the wire balusters of the railing jangle as she started up after me.

It wasn't until I began pawing through her

drawers that she really started to let loose. Suddenly I was glad that I had the vodka with my breakfast as it numbed me from the screaming and, when started I pulling out clothes from the wardrobe in the bedroom, the slapping. Sophie wasn't a tiny girl, so as much as I wanted to play the hard man in this I found myself hurrying along with the first armload as strata of bruises formed along my back and shoulders. The only consolation that I had is that being angrily yelled at by an Italian woman while she slaps at you is strangely erotic.

Getting out Sophie's door, up the stairs, and through our apartment entry while holding onto what clothing I could and being assaulted was tricky. It required some strategic body blocking and the use of all of my limbs, which made me glad that I had prehensile toes. Between Sophie's vigorous yelling and the swearing that was building up in of my throat, we made quite a scene by the time I actually got us into apartment #5.

Whatever cuteness or novelty there was in being slapped on by this tall, blonde Italian had worn off by the time I got us in. I threw down the first load of clothing right on top of Cheryl. Her eyes shot open and she scanned the unmentionables that had landed in her lap. Her stupefied expression slowly rotated from there, to me, to Sophie. The last of those was clearly demanding in angry Italian what Cheryl was going to do about the fact that her husband had lost his God damned mind.

Coming round back to me Cheryl stated dryly, "This ... is not what I meant."

Going back to playing the hard man, I just grunted and said, "You explain it to her," and headed back towards the door. But Sophie was having none of it – she imposed herself directly in my path and moved to intercept when I tried to step around her. She bent her neck and shoulders like an angry snake, trying to catch my gaze, demanding some explanation. I wondered, then, what happened to that frightened woman who had hidden behind my couch just the other day.

"What the Hell did they do to you?" I said, without thinking. I was fairly sure that Sophie didn't understand it, but maybe she had heard the phrase enough to get the gist because she stopped, stood up straight, and blinked those big green eyes at me. Cheryl spoke up in calm, reassuring Italian from behind me, causing Sophie to shift her gaze to the couch. I used the opportunity to slip by her, heading back out the door and down the stairs.

I spent a few minutes reconnoitering the small place. I wanted to figure out what Sophie might need, but also try to figure out what type of person she was. Any contraband laying around might tell me if she had any bad habits.

I didn't find anything. I found a kitchen that was spartan and somehow well appointed at the same time. The refrigerator, blender, and under-cabinet microwave were all of the same white plastic and chrome style, probably bought as a part of the same set. The remains of a grapefruit lay on a white, plastic cutting board on the counter, a brushed metal knife laying next to it. I checked the fridge to find a mostly full bottle of white wine, which I took. There were also more fruits and meats, some of which I recognized from the other day, all in a state of being half-eaten.

I uncorked the bottle and stepped back into the living room. Belting some of the weak wine, I took a close look at the room for the first time. It was furnished much like ours, with a couch across from the entrance, flanked on the opposite side by two

One Sore Rib

chairs, all of it arranged around a wooden coffee table. On the wall the couch faced there was a fireplace instead of a television, with two tall windows on either side. There were no pictures on the mantle and nothing hanging on the wall above it. I wandered over to the bookcase that was opposite the kitchen. It was full of well-thumbed books of the type that you find in hotel lobbies, ranging from obscure out-of-print titles to famous writers whose copyrights had expired.

As I looked through the bookcase the window seemed to jump in my peripheral vision, paranoia tugging at the corner of my eyes. I tried to ignore it, but then a restlessness started in me until I couldn't resist walking over. I peeked through the curtain out at Calle de Preti, a narrow street that would give no place to hide if the Kid and the Old Man were out below. I stared out for a few minutes and began to wonder if they might have friends or, if they were working for the Verdicchio guy Dennis had mentioned, how he might have other thugs on his roster. If either of those were true than I wouldn't be able to recognize any new players.

I felt the paranoia start to turn from a tug into a vortex. I shook it off with another pull of the bottle and went back to the front of the apartment and up the spiral staircase that snaked out of the floor next to the entry door.

After bumping my head at the top of the stairs I wondered how Sophie lived with the low ceilings of the second floor. I cursed quietly as I thought about this, then took another swig of the bottle as if it might dull the pain. The upper floor was the same dark wood as the rest of the apartment, with the same white painted walls. Off the stairwell the corridor turned to the left where it formed a short, narrow hallway with two doorways springing off its sides opposite one another. It ended at a set of glass doors that led outside.

At the same end of the hallway as the stairs was a chest of drawers that I had ignored before in the rush to her room. I set the bottle on top of it to rummage through them only to find it completely empty.

Walking the short, narrow corridor it creaked and groaned with every step. To the left was what appeared to be a laundry room with the tiniest washer and dryer I had ever seen in my life, including on ship. Unlike the kitchen, the machines here looked abused, kicked and scuffed. The front-loading door of the washing machine, which wasn't bigger than the circumference of a swab bucket, was beaten and chipped.

Reversing course took me across the hall and into the bedroom again. Taking a longer moment to inspect it I saw the bed was a decent size, almost a queen, sitting on a wooden frame with white sheets dressed tight against the mattress. Above the bed was a sizable window with a wooden shutter covering it, hinged at the top with a peg at the bottom so it could be propped open. In another moment of paranoia I pushed open the shutter and looked out to see that her bedroom window was directly over the entrance to the building.

The bedroom also had a bathroom off of it, with a shower that was enclosed in glass, a sink that was so low to the floor that it seemed impossible to use, and a toilet with another porcelain throne next to it. The odd knobs on the second one marked it as something Cheryl had told me was called a bidet.

Out of all the rooms in the house the bathroom one showed the most signs of use. Light spatterings of water were on the shower with a toothbrush and hairbrush uncomfortably sharing the wet surface of the sink together. There was enough dirt and other nasty in the grout between the floor tiles to suggest that the room didn't get enough air circulation for the amount of use it saw.

Leaving the bedroom, I walked to the end of the hall and pushed the drapes aside to peek through the glass doors. Outside was a small balcony, barely big enough to sit two people, with a round wrought-iron table and two chairs. There were some pots for plants but if there had been anything living in them they had long since died.

The tiny balcony faced out on the same street as the window I had peeked out of downstairs. I moved to open it, but something stopped me. More than just the itching paranoia from before, it was a choking fear that hit me so quickly that I retreated backward from the door like something was about to punch through from the other side. After a moment of standing a few feet away from it, I felt a kick-myself embarrassment. I was nearly 100% certain they didn't have snipers in Venice, but I didn't want to step outside on that balcony.

I took another pull from the bottle, nearly draining it, and realized I was shaking. Embarrassed or not, I walked away from the door, giving it one last suspicious and shamed glare.

Back downstairs I sat on the coffee table and shook out my hands, trying to exorcise whatever was rattling me. What had started out as me searching Sophie's place had turned into walking the perimeter. I hadn't done that since my first nights home.

I finished off the bottle. I blinked sweat from my eyes and shook my head, then got up to go in the kitchen. I raided the fridge, taking a few pieces of fruit, chewing on them slowly in the hopes they might get the alcohol smell off my breath. When I stopped shaking I found a suitcase underneath the bed upstairs and filled it with clothes.

By the time I came back up the main stairs and into our apartment most of the anger, thankfully, seemed to have passed. Sophie was sitting on the edge of the coffee table, bent over at the waist, leaning towards my wife on the couch whispering something that I couldn't hear. She looked up when she saw me enter, shot up standing and stormed over in such a hurry I thought I was wrong about the anger passing and about to get a slap. Instead she snatched the bag from me, turned around, walked back to the coffee table, dropped it, and popped it open.

Taking out a white, sheer blouse she held it up by the shoulders and clucked at it sympathetically as if it were a child. She continued to do this with each piece of clothing, taking it out, examining it, then folding and laying it on the coffee table, interspersing each one with dirty looks in my direction.

After I was sure I was safe I walked into the living room until I was standing at the back of the couch. Looking down, Cheryl was there and she gave me a warm but cryptic smile. Even with her fatigue, it had a hint of the mischievousness I had seen the night she had banished me from our Venetian apartment.

"She's going to stay."

Chapter 10

What followed next, even with everything that happened afterward, I still tend to think of as the good days.

I got up in the morning before the women and started coffee. The two had stayed up late talking the night before, Cheryl having me carry her upstairs so she could show Sophie the incredibly small spare bedroom. Then, with Cheryl propped up against what passed for a headboard on the bed, the two of them jawed as Sophie moved her things in. Her unpacking complete, they indicated the bed sheets and walls as if talking about Sophie's options for decorating. Or at least that's how it seemed to me, standing on the outside of the language barrier. It probably says more about me than Sophie that I thought she'd fret about having to downgrade in the size of her bedroom, but she appeared more disappointed in not having her own bath. It was little things like that that reminded me she was a stranger.

Their conversation made for less than exciting viewing, though. Eventually, somewhat amazed that Cheryl was still awake, I kissed her good night, said goodbye to Sophie, and went to the other bedroom. As Cheryl's nocturnal rest had become less and less like sleep, she had been staying in the same bed as me less often. So I had, unfortunately, become accustomed to sleeping alone.

But then morning came. With the two women not yet awake the absence of Italian filled the apartment with its own void, magnified by the gray light and sound of rain pattering against the windows. It was the kind of quiet that made me feel like a lumbering beast, made all the more fragile by the thickness my hangover. Fortunately, with both of them upstairs, I didn't have to worry about sneaking around anyone resting on the couch.

While I struggled with brewing coffee I leaned against the Formica kitchen counter and tried to rub the fatigue and the aftermath of alcohol out of my eyes. Like so much else in Venice, the coffee pot was strange and foreign, a small, bow tie shaped piece of chrome that sat on the stove top and silently percolated coffee from water in its bottom to a thick sludge in its top. By the time I got the first cup of coffee in me, my disquiet with the quiet had resolved itself into a kind of appreciation of the peace.

With caffeine in me, I decided to take stock of our supplies, which I found to be dangerously low. There were the few bits of fruit and meat brought from Sophie's, enough OJ to cover the bottom of the bottle, and not much else. Leaving had bothered me before, but now with Sophie here and thoughts of the Old Man and the Kid out there somewhere in Venice, I almost worried too much to go. The Old Man and the Kid didn't seem the type to be out this early though. If they were and decided to push a confrontation with me, there was a part of me that welcomed it.

Bumping into the pair on the street wasn't what concerned me, but them coming up when I was out. Sipping on my second cup of mud, I walked around the room. There were windows, but on the third floor they would make for difficult points of entry. The one door out into the hall was a thick-bodied slab, one that looked like it would fit right into a James Bond movie and it could probably stop the bullets to match. So unless the Kid and the Old Man enjoyed rappelling in their spare time, had a helicopter or a battering ram, I was fairly certain Cheryl and Sophie would be safe while I was gone.

I went upstairs to let Cheryl know I was going out. I never left her without saying goodbye, although she often wasn't conscious enough these days to recognize my departure. But a gentle kiss often drew some muttering from her and the bittersweet warmth that gave was good enough.

This morning I found Cheryl lying on the guest bed with Sophie sleeping in a plush chair she had pulled up next to it. I stood in the doorway for what felt like a very long time, not sure how to feel about any of this. If I had to paint a picture of everything good and bad about Sophie being here, this would be it: The comfort her presence brought to Cheryl, and by extension, me, but also the other, confusing emotions she drug up that I didn't want to deal with. Not least of which was the quiet anticipation of waiting for the other shoe to drop. I wondered when Cheryl might ask Sophie about the Old Man and the Kid.

With that question on my mind, I couldn't think of a better time to escape. I grabbed my coat and headed out into the sea of umbrellas and tarps that made up the Venice's main thoroughfares that day. It was a decent walk, on the north side of the San Marco sestiere, where the apartment was on the south, but I decided to head to the Rialto Market, which always had the best selection of fresh fruits for Cheryl's slurries.

It was a simple place, with wooden and plastic crates propping up the boxes of fruits and vegetables, each one with a small, hand-drawn sign indicating what was in it and its price. I stepped under the orange tarp they had stretched over the market on days it rained, which was as often as not, and started hunting for the best picks. The stagnated smell of the canal mixed with the dirt on the vegetables and the rain on the cobblestones to form a pervading odor that was earthy and surprisingly pleasant. It made the market one of my favorite places.

Haggling with the merchants did not. Unlike other foreign cities I had been to, including ones where people had been actively trying to kill me, the merchants of Venice despised it when I attempted to converse with them in their native tongue. If I started in Italian, the response always came in English. Continuing to try Italian was met with an open hostility that would have made me reach for my rifle in other parts of the world. I had learned to accept this after the first few days. I never did pick up any Italian practicing it with the locals.

The one exception was an older merchant I bought oranges from. He was always wrapped in a fur-lined windbreaker against the rain, his large nose poking out from behind a pair of ever-present sunglasses. I guess I had been around his booth enough times to be recognized as something more permanent than a daytripper. He was the only one to give me a smile.

So I thanked him and scooped up what I wanted and counted out my Euros and headed to the grocery store for the rest of the supplies. The quickest way there, though, was across the Rialto Bridge, the ancient white stone pedestrian walkway that spanned the Grand Canal. It was covered in its own batch of shops, small booth-like structures that sold everything from Rolexes to plastic masks. But even at this early hour it was already packed with tourists. I considered taking a water taxi to avoid the crowds, but felt how few Euros I had jangling in my pocket and thought better of it.

The grocery store was one of a chain named Billa, someone's attempt to make a 21st century supermarket in the middle of a 14th century town. It managed to combine the worst of both, with the fluorescent lighting and artificial plastic of the former but with the space and selection of the latter. I can't imagine how much the store's yellow and red sign, which hung outside on a marble face of what might have once been an artisan's shop, must have offended the locals. No surprise then the place felt like the epicenter for Venetians' hatred of outsiders. I squeezed my way through its aisles and corners to get what we needed and puzzled my way through the narrow maze of the checkout line as quick as I could. I only paused when counting out my cash gave me concrete facts on how little remained. It didn't help my attitude.

    Maybe that's why, with my arms full of groceries, on my walk south back to the apartment I started to feel that increasingly familiar itch of suspicion. I considered how vulnerable I was with both of my hands tied up carrying bags. Even if the Kid and Old Man confronted me directly rather than ambushing me from behind, I probably couldn't untangle myself fast enough to mount a decent defense. So I hurried back, jangling keys and cursing through the front door, up the stairs, and into apartment #5.

    Cheryl and Sophie may have been late risers, or at least they were by service standards, but Sophie was awake when I walked in, busying herself with tiding up the place. She poked her head out from the kitchen and, seeing the bags, rewarded me with a smile. That smile made me forget for a moment that I had been fleeing perhaps not-so-imaginary phantoms, made me forget that I was cold and wet. She disappeared into the kitchen again and appeared a moment later holding the last of the OJ. Taking one of the bags, she put the glass into that now empty hand and took the other bag while I sipped on the juice to cover an

One Sore Rib

uneasy grin.

Sophie headed back into the kitchen, leaving a trail of bouncy Italian behind her. A second later she turned around again, maybe to ask me something about breakfast. But I had already downed the OJ and was halfway up the stairs, moving fast enough to cause the wire railing to sound like someone had thrown a guitar down the spiral.

I told myself that Sophie and I had nothing to talk about and no way to discuss it, that I was going up to get Cheryl. But I knew I was just getting away from her. Part of it was that I was attracted to her, yes, and that even with the language barrier she still had an effervescent smile that could make me feel as if my tongue was swollen and my skin flush. I couldn't tell if she was flirting with me or just genuinely warm, or both, and I didn't know which made me more uncomfortable. Putting that aside, her presence brought a small piece of happiness into our lives when I felt all that I should be is miserable. The mere alleviation of this produced its own kind of guilt by-product.

Halting the escape velocity that had launched me up the stairs I paused at the door of the bedroom Cheryl lay in. Sound asleep on her side, the blankets looked as if they covered a child instead of a full-grown woman. Walking in I peeled off the wet layers of my clothes while kicking off my shoes, not wanting to get her damp as I slid into the bed behind her. I wrapped my arms around her and pulled her to my chest. Trying to ignore how thin and frail she felt, I concentrated on transferring my body heat to her, knowing how she was almost always cold these days. Her body shifted against mine, announcing dawning consciousness, and I held her tighter as I felt her shoulder blades dig into my chest.

I could feel her smile as she gently rubbed her chin against my arm, "How's my furnace?"

"Good," I smiled at the old, inside joke. "I went out and picked up some breakfast." I could feel her crinkle her nose, the repugnance she felt as clear to me as my heat signature was to her. In an attempt to placate I added, "I think Sophie's going to put something together."

"Hurmm," came the reply indicating that Sophie's enthusiasm in the kitchen wasn't going to change Cheryl's view on breakfast. I just held her that much closer and shushed her.

I nuzzled my nose into the peach fuzz that covered the back of her head, tracing some unknown semaphore of affection into her skull. After a moment of this I did some nose-crinkling of my own. "You need a bath."

"I need to go to the bathroom too." Even after weeks of me taking care of her most basic needs, I could feel Cheryl's shame telegraph through her body. I had found the best thing for her dignity was to ignore her embarrassment, so I slid out of the bed then picked her up to take her into our bathroom. One likely outcome of this adventure to the head was me getting wet in some fashion, so I didn't bother putting my clothes back on.

I sat her on the toilet. Cheryl slumped down on the seat, leaning against the porcelain sink next to it that was close enough to act as a handy buttress. After sleeping all night she still seemed exhausted and I worried that I had made a mistake in letting her stay up late. Raising her head, she read the concern on my face and, not so tired as to not be able to glare, gave me a burning proud stare and shooed me out. Cheryl had always refused to share the bathroom when one of us was doing our business, all the way back to the apartment we had shared as newlyweds, which had been smaller than the Venetian one.

I went into the bedroom, pretending to find clothes to wear once all of this was done. That didn't exhaust enough time for Cheryl to finish up, so I picked up a book of poetry that she had been keeping on her nightstand. I flipped through it to find:

> *Daughters are never shot*
> *from a forehead fully formed.*
> *Father's labors are for naught,*
> *save that little girls are born.*

Those words put a disquiet in my stomach that I could not move. I sat with them there on the bed for awhile.

Cheryl called, "I'm done."

I stepped to the bathroom door and leaned against the frame. She was still sitting on the throne, which told me she was too weak today to get up herself. Rather than worry her with more of my worry, I just asked, as nonchalantly as I could, "So, bath or sponge?"

With a Herculean effort Cheryl raised her head, her shoulders so bowed it was nearly between her knees. "Bath," she replied. The rings under her eyes made me worry that much more, so I hid it by walking to the basin and turning on the faucet. I felt the water for temperature for a few minutes without saying anything.

"You OK?"

The flood of responses that came up to Cheryl's question wouldn't have helped any, particular my honest desire for a drink. Struggling for an answer that wasn't a lie but didn't waste time on the pointless, I spied an odd bit of Americana on the bathtub sill.

Picking it up between thumb and forefinger I put the rubber fowl near her face. "I'm just ducky," I said, squeaking it for good measure.

"Idiot," she said, her eyes squinting with the pain of the pun, or the beginning of a reluctant laugh. It was hard to say which.

I smirked at the insult, stood up and asked, "Ready?"

She nodded her head warily. Sliding one arm behind her back and the other under her legs, I moved her into the bath. She made several quick inhalations telling me the water was a bit too hot, but then eased into it with a comfortable sigh.

With her eyes closed in what I hoped was relaxation, I looked at her body as I rarely did these days. My eyes moved across it, down the ruin of her chest with its angry scars, to the knolls of her ribs and abdomen, down to the barren valley between her legs. And I wished I could kiss her there without embarrassing her, bring her back to life like some miracle Lothario, causing her to blossom and take me in as she had so many times before.

A splash landed on my face and chest, causing me to sputter, blinking out of my thoughts. "This ain't no peep show," Cheryl said, trying to smile through the discomfort being stared at always brought her these days.

My response of, "Hey, I can pay," got me another splash and the duty of having to mop up the wet floor later. The damage already done, I splashed her back and we played back and forth like that for a few seconds. I think she might have giggled.

Sputtering with a face full of water from her final assault, I surrendered. I toweled off my chest then went to get her clothes.

Cheryl had never unpacked. She never unpacked

One Sore Rib

on any trip we had ever taken, insisting it was a waste of time. So I leaned down to get her suitcase out from under the bed and began rummaging through it to find something that I thought might be appropriate for the day. Staring out the open shutter above the bed, I tried to guess the weather, as I was already thinking about taking her up to the rooftop garden later.

Trying to decipher what the gray clouds outside the window might mean for the future, I felt a burning at the back of my head. The paranoia that had been returning lately rolled down my neck and shoulders as I slowly pulled myself to a full attention. I spun around like a man trying to catch a ghost.

Sophie stood in the hall, just beyond the bedroom door, either on her way to her own bedroom or to check on the noise Cheryl and I had been making, staring at me in all of my naked ape glory. My quick movement towards her caused her to jump a bit, with a quick inhalation of breath. But nothing else.

I didn't move, my eyelids the only part of me responding to cranial commands, blinking. It didn't help my paralysis that Sophie didn't reverse course, or excuse herself, or do any of the things I thought she'd do at any moment, but stood there, blushing furiously.

"Hey cabana boy," Cheryl called from the bath, "bring me my towel!" I snapped my head away from Sophie to the direction of Cheryl's voice, tried to say something and failed, then saw in that second Sophie had disappeared, leaving only the afterimage of her in my mind.

I did what any sane man would do in that situation – I pretended it didn't happen. Throwing the gown I had pulled out of the suitcase over my shoulder, I went back into the bathroom where Cheryl had already started to drain the tub. After drying and dressing her I laid her on the bed while I dressed myself. Walking with her was tricky down the narrow spiral staircase, but I made my way, scouting it out with my toes, moving with short, curving steps that made me feel like a ballerina.

Still blushing, but smiling, Sophie waved at us from the kitchen as I laid Cheryl down on the couch. While I propped her up with pillows, Cheryl smiled back and greeted her weakly. I studiously avoided eye contact with anyone.

I handed Cheryl the remote and sat down on the couch at her feet. Then, as she did almost inevitably every morning, she turned on that strange creature she was so fascinated with, Italian television. Not as strange as the TV I had seen on stopovers in Germany, it still contained more noise, enthusiasm, and nudity than anything I had ever seen in America. All the men were old and all the women were young and beautiful, but from what little I had gathered, that was how most things worked in Italian society. After a few days of watching this, the kind of residual anger I could feel walking around Venice and, I imagined, all of Italy, made a little more sense.

I could feel my own anger building up as we sat there. I couldn't stand watching its jabbering and arm-waving, but I knew complaining about the idiocy on the screen would only upset Cheryl and ruin her enjoyment of it. She watched it like an anthropologist, snapping mental pictures of Italian culture with each show.

I stayed rooted on the couch, though, trying desperately to pretend that Sophie and whatever delicious things I could smell coming from the kitchen didn't exist. As my frustration grew with each jiggling bounce and sideways grin from the television, I began to beat myself up over the stupidity of my own trap.

Fine, whatever, she had seen me naked. Lots of women had seen me naked. OK, maybe not a lot, but many. Well, a few. But it was time to put on the big boy pants and deal with this like an adult. Also, I was hungry.

Moving Cheryl's feet off of me to get up, I saw she had already fallen asleep again. I squeezed her foot, still warm from the heat of the bath, and went to the threshold of the kitchen. Sophie had her back to me, dancing minutely to some tune she was humming, working at the cutting board. For a moment I admired the shape of her again and wondered to myself if I had the chance to see her as she had seen me, would I take it?

I cleared my throat. Sophie turned, a bit surprised, the noise of the television having covered my approach. For a long second, she stood rigid, eyes wide, clearly unsure of herself. I only raised my eyebrows and frowned with my cheeks puffed out in what I hoped was an embarrassed and chastised manner.

Sophie laughed, a good and honest laugh that made me smile and took whatever shame or guilt I might have felt and made it seem silly. Seeing me smile only made her laugh that much more, a good sidesplitting laugh that made my smile into its own laughter. It went on long enough until my belly ached and we were both trying to catch our breath.

I wiped a tear from my eye and pointed to the bag of fruit on the counter. Sophie gestured at it with the knife in her hand and nodded, moving to the left to give me room. She giggled again as I stepped next to her.

I began the morning ritual of making Cheryl's slurry, taking each fruit out that I needed and placing them into the blender. Sophie continued to slice on the cutting board, side-glances at me as I worked. I took out the peach, bananas, and strawberries, putting in a little OJ. It certainly smelled a lot better than the slurries I used to make her with carrots and beets, before we had given up.

And with that thought, it was good to have someone there, another body in the kitchen. The bones in me grew heavier, weighing my shoulders and head down, and the peach that had been headed towards the blender ended up resting on the counter. I felt like a stalled car, gravity holding me in place.

The only thing that penetrated this hole was the impression of Sophie glancing at me with increasing frequency. A compulsion to appear normal, to pretend everything was fine, pushed me to get moving, but whatever embarrassment or social more leaned on me to move, it was unsuccessful.

The tip of the knife Sophie was holding penetrated the tunnel of my vision and I snapped to, blinking my eyes. Her face held a gentle smile, her left hand holding some sort of spriggy, green herb while her right pointed the knife at the peach. It took me a second to realize she had asked me a question.

I blinked again, shaking off my torpor. "Sorry, what?"

"Come si chiama quel frutto?" It was pleasant and musical as her voice tended to be, and with the morning light coming into the kitchen from the windows behind her, she was beautiful to look at. And I had absolutely no idea what she was saying.

I shook my head again, feeling that embarrassment from before begin to gain a toehold, "I'm sorry, what?"

She put the knife and twig down on the cutting board, then picked up the peach from the counter, holding it between us as if displaying it for a class and said simply, "Frutto."

"Oh, right," the embarrassment had enough of a grip now to cause my cheeks to flush. "Yeah, fruit, right."

She moved the peach slightly to indicate she was still speaking about it, "Come si chiama?"

I looked down at the peach, then up at her, finding her green eyes difficult to escape. "It's a peach," then reiterated simply, "Peach."

She gave me a wry grin and said, "Pesca."

We went on like that for a bit, back and forth at first with the fruit, laughing a bit when we discovered the word for banana in Italian is banana, which, funnily, is a feminine word ('la' instead of 'el'). After each fruit had been bilingually pronounced, I added it to the blender, and the lesson also became an impromptu one in how to make Cheryl's breakfast. Then we went onto the things on her cutting board, which now that I paid attention to it, looked delicious.

The inventory of the kitchen counter catalogued in English and Italian I hit the blender's On switch, killing the conversation. I ground the fruit, added a bit more juice, ground again, until the consistency was right. Finished, I pulled out a cup and straw, sliding the contents of the blender in.

Pronouncing it done by holding up the cup of pulverized fruit, Sophie bent her frame as if to curtsey, bringing her hands up next to her face in faux-applause. She then bent down to retrieve a skillet from one of the cabinets under the counter, and moved to reached around me to grab the bow-tie coffee peculator from the oven. With heavy metal in each hand she ushered me out of the kitchen, making what sounded like some kind of promises.

Cheryl was still asleep on the couch when I set the slurry down and sat next to her. Taking the remote, I turned down the Italian splaying out of the TV. This, naturally, caused her to roll over, blink some kind of awareness into her blue eyes, and then poked at me with her toes. "Was watching that," she said simply. I gave her a look that she must have interpreted correctly because she blinked at me and groused, "Don't give me that look."

I rolled my eyes for her benefit, then handed her the remote. The television, not surprisingly, had an old man with slicked-back hair in a suit so fine it might have glowed, sitting next to a beautiful brunette in a dress cut low enough that I amused myself for a few minutes wondering if she were going to pop out of it. The two of them were speaking to a third woman who, I gathered, was an actress from Brazil and clearly had been chosen as an exotic alternative to the parade of beauties that inhabited Italian networks.

If this had been America I might have been able to pacify myself with the usual "fight for the right to say whatever you blah blah blah" speech, but it wasn't. The only thing that translated through the stream of nonsense was the forced jocularity of it and all that pointlessness shredded my nerves like a cheese grater. As the minutes dragged on I started to feel that irrational anger grow behind my eyes and a headache grow with it. I pinched the bridge of my nose and tried to blink it away. But it just kept coming until I felt I was restraining myself from putting a foot into the television, or snapping the remote away from Cheryl with an angry comment. Or maybe just getting up from the couch and screaming before I hurled myself out the window.

Instead I just comforted myself with the mild torture of pushing the slurry on Cheryl and insisting she eat. She grumbled about that too, but at least tried to look like she was eating, pushing the straw around with her tongue.

Sophie came into the living room, holding a plate of something that smelled wonderful. With a word or five in Italian, she set it down and I could see that it was what looked like a pile of tiny sausages, shaped like pancakes and dotted with red herbs. Unsure of the proper etiquette I had to restrain myself from reaching out, grabbing one and shoving it in my mouth.

That impulse was killed immediately as the smell of the food hit Cheryl and she vomited into the bucket I kept next to her for just such emergencies. I bent to the task of consoling her while Sophie and the offending plate both disappeared. It went on for several minutes.

There wasn't anything to be done but for me to put my hand on her back, trying to rub some comfort into her as I steadied her on the couch, keeping her from falling onto the floor, or worse, into the bucket. Finished, she painfully rolled onto her back, shrinking into the sofa, pulling the purple blanket around herself. I wiped her mouth and murmured things I hoped were reassuring. Then, exhausted by the contortions of emptying herself, Cheryl passed into a deep sleep that made me worried until I could see the regular movements of her breathing.

After I was sure she was unconscious I took the bucket into the kitchen, emptying it into the sink and washing it out. Sophie was sitting at the tiny table at the other end of the kitchen, having made herself so small that I had forgotten she was there. She didn't say anything, but her eyes spoke volumes of guilt and worry. I could only say, "It's OK. You didn't know," and variations of that until at least the gentleness of my tone made it clear no one was upset.

Abashedly, she gestured to the plate of sausages on the butcher block as if she were afraid to bring up the offending meats again. I nodded enthusiastically though, the vomit unable to put me off my hunger. Clearly pleased by this, she swept up and, taking my arm by the hand and elbow, sat me at the small table, followed by the sausages, a few small pastries, cups of coffee and juice. Sitting down opposite me she indicated the feast with her eyes, imploring me to dig in. I did so earnestly, without hesitation or regret. It was the best meal I'd had in I don't know how long.

The sausages tasted of salt and pepper, and something pungent I couldn't place, and it offset the sweetness of the juice and pastries in a way that made me want to eat faster than I really ought. My mouth full of goodness, I stopped and looked up at Sophie, feeling myself blush again. Her features said she was surprised at my excitement for the meal, but then just laughed at seeing me cheeks plumped out.

I slowed down, picking over my next piece of sausage more carefully, feeling an obligation to use utensils this time rather than snatching it up with my fingers. Sophie poured herself a cup of coffee, sat down at the table across from me, and crossed her legs, causing the light material of her dress to billow slightly in a way that was hard to ignore. Interlacing her fingers, she rested her hands on her raised knee and watched me eat. This caused me to slow down further, chewing the remaining mouthfuls in deliberate bites. Eventually she stopped staring at me, turning her head to stare out the frosted glass of the window in the kitchen's south wall. I'm not sure what made me more uncomfortable.

The discomfort might have been mutual. After a time, smoothing the front of her skirt with her hands, Sophie stood up and excused herself with a few words. Grateful to have a moment alone, I continued to eat.

I heard the television volume go down again and after a time Sophie speaking, just loud enough to be heard over the television. To my surprise I heard Cheryl's quiet responses, the two of them talking about what sounded like nothing but the mundane. I finished up my fourth sausage, ate down a pastry, then took my cup of coffee and walked to the threshold of the kitchen.

I stood there drinking it, Sophie sitting on the couch blocking my view of Cheryl and hers of me, watching them without feeling observed myself. Culinary efforts that induced vomiting aside, Cheryl was more active around Sophie, that couldn't be denied. I could see Cheryl's hand moving out beyond the lip of the couch and Sophie's profile to point at the television, indicating whatever she was speaking about. Sophie's responses, the smile clear in her voice, harmonized with Cheryl's in a way that had nothing to do with any concern for the Beast or his Master.

Standing at the room's edge, I felt a biting jealously. I just couldn't talk to her like that anymore.

Feeling spiteful, but doing it anyway, I walked up to Cheryl behind the couch and smiled down at her, which she ably returned, causing me to feel another spike of jealousy. We exchanged our ritualized "Heys" and I asked her if she wanted to go up to the roof. She peered out the window and saw that the clouds from earlier had given way to blue skies and said, "Sure."

I picked her up, blankets and all, and took her up the spiral stairs and then the outside ones, Sophie trailing behind us and picking up whatever Cheryl may have dropped along the way. With the sun out the terrace and the whole of Venice were no longer dreary, the terracotta tiles of the roofs shining in burning oranges and deep browns, the white facades of buildings almost too bright to look at. But the cool touch of the wind was just enough to keep it from getting too warm and brought the briny smell of the ocean with it. The combination of all these things made a pleasant, anesthetic cocktail for all of us. We spent hours up on the roof top garden terrace without doing or saying much.

Eventually, not even the peace of the Venetian skyline could hold off my worries and I started to become concerned that Cheryl was getting too much sun. I walked over to her lying on the bench, blocking the sun as I smiled down at her and said, "Let's go." She just smiled up at me, eyes squinting from the light, and replied, "Okay."

I took her back down, followed by the shadow of Sophie, and Cheryl went back onto the couch and back on went the TV. The relaxation from earlier somehow made the Italian television more bearable and I drifted off.

I was roused out of dozing in a chair near the couch by Cheryl's voice. I blinked awake and looked over at her looking at me. "What?" I asked, bleary-eyed, meaning that I hadn't understood her.

"Sophie's asking if she can go down to her place and grab a few other things." While I was dozing Cheryl had rearranged herself so she was on her back with the top of her head towards me, putting her face upside-down. Above and behind her, in a chair on the opposite end of the couch from me, Sophie sat looking at me with a sheepish grin. It was the first time Sophie had spoken to me through Cheryl. It made me feel awkward in a way that made me push myself out of my chair and answer in the affirmative just to have something to do.

The ether of the afternoon burned off at the touch of paranoia that the prospect of leaving the apartment brought. I cleared each area in succession (stairhead, stairwell, second floor, apartment) before letting Sophie follow me. She stopped every time I held up my hand, rigid, then driftingly followed me when I summoned her forward.

Once inside, I expected her to head up to the bedroom or bathroom, but she went to the kitchen. I followed her in to see her loading a bag with spices and other seasonings. Finished with that she opened up a bottom cabinet away from the stove and took out two bottles, one looked like wine, the other a clear liquor, and held them up for my inspection.

"Sure, bring those," I said, trying to sound like I didn't care.

Repeating the previous operation in reverse, we headed back to apartment #5 where Sophie returned to the kitchen, putting everything she had brought away. There were some sausages left and I nibbled on those as a substitute for the lunch we had all dozed through as Sophie went to work on dinner.

I walked back to the living room, sitting next to Cheryl. She stopped watching the television to give me a smile. "She making dinner?"

I shrugged in an attempt to appear indifferent. "I guess."

She poked me with a toe until I turned to her. "Isn't this nice?" she asked, the expression on her face making it clear what answer she wanted.

"Sure, yeah," I sort-of lied, unsure how I felt about the entire thing. While the noises and smells Sophie was making in the kitchen made me happy, her presence made things complicated. Before her arrival everything had its place and the end was preordained and now only the worst parts of the future felt certain.

Sophie eventually came out with a vegetable soup that was much less fragrant than the sausages, which was maybe how she got Cheryl to eat a little. Even as a confirmed meat-eater, I had to admit it was damned tasty.

After the meal Sophie turned on some television show that had both her and Cheryl in stitches. I broke open the bottle of clear liquor and drank myself into a contented numbness. Not long after the sun went down Sophie realized she was laughing alone and switched off the television while I carried Cheryl up to our bed.

I woke up in the dark with my face wet. Thinking it had started to rain I began to get up to close the shutter on the window. In doing so I nearly ran into Cheryl's face with my own, her barely-there weight on me as she gazed down at me. She was crying.

"You poor, stupid man. What are you still doing here?"

I blinked, taken aback by the question, and then raised a hand to take her cheek in my palm, wiping the tears from it with my thumb. As if she could no longer support herself, she put the weight of her head in my hand, letting me hold her up. I thought about her question for a long time in the dark; if maybe I would have been better off if she had died quickly, or if I had just left her to die on her own, or had killed her out in the Australian desert, or any of the other things that had crossed my mind out of stupidity or desperation or just pure, black selfishness. When I had thought about all of those things honestly, I caressed her cheek with my thumb again and said, "You're my girl."

She cried more then and I held her tight and we stayed like that till morning.

Chapter 11

We fell into a routine pretty quickly after that. For a while everyday was a lot like the first day.

As much as I hoped she would Cheryl didn't ask Sophie anything about herself or the Old Man and the Kid. She didn't ask a lot of questions of people in life. She just wasn't that kind of person and I think some people loved that about her. But there was a part of me that thought she was torturing me by not trying to find out at least something about Sophie's situation. After my conversation with Dennis I had my suspicions, but I desperately wanted to know.

After a day or two of shopping before the women got up Sophie caught up with me the night before an outing. She handed me a slip of paper with an expectant smile and a happy gleam in her eye. I read over it – some of the items I recognized, some of them I didn't – but it was clear enough that it was a shopping list. After the sausages and soup, I was more than happy to get her whatever she wanted for the kitchen. So I smiled at her and held the list between thumb and forefinger and waved it in a gesture that I hoped was positive. I tried not to think about how little money was left or what I would do when it finally ran out.

From the couch and through the blare of the Italian coming out of the television Cheryl still recognized the worry I was trying to hide. "What's that?"

"Looks like a shopping list."

"Something wrong?"

"No," I lied, "there's just some things on it that I don't recognize."

Without lifting herself up from the couch, she gestured me to her, spinning a hand on her wrist, drawing a wheel in the air that motioned towards her. "Give it."

I sat on the coffee table near Cheryl's head while Sophie settled down at her feet and we began another impromptu language lesson. Cheryl asked me what I didn't recognize and then told me what it was, had me repeat it, and then did the same with Sophie, but in English. Cheryl then asked Sophie which ingredient was for what or how they went together and had her try to explain it to me, with me stopping her for questions. She let us both do as much talking as we could before reaching a linguistic impasse that required her to intervene. The durations in which Cheryl said nothing became longer and longer until we realized she was asleep. I smiled ruefully over at Sophie and was struck by the sadness on her face, an expression that she only let show when she thought Cheryl wasn't paying attention.

I kissed Cheryl on the head then and picked her up to put her to bed. Upstairs, I sat on the bed with her for awhile then sighed heavily as I realized that I wasn't the least bit tired. Even if I did crawl into bed with her she most likely wouldn't know it. More often than not her sleep these days resembled a coma or a more permanent, deeper kind of sleep.

I got up and went downstairs to pull a bottle out of the cabinet and a Peroni out of the fridge. Exiting the kitchen I realized Sophie was still awake and, really for the first time, we were alone. I hesitated in the threshold between the two rooms, holding beverages in both hands, each deadlier than the last. I felt a bit ashamed at having someone witness what passed as my coping mechanism. Surely, my time and what little of our money remained could be better spent.

There was no judgment from Sophie, though. She just picked up the remote and, in a slow exaggerated fashion, switched off the television. With a wink and a flash the TV was off and the room dark and quiet, all the gibbering Italian gone. She smiled at me, gesturing at the now dead set with a flourish of her palms like a show model or a magician. The silence of the room was stark and I became very uncomfortable.

I stood there until Sophie patted the couch next to her, getting up herself, leaving a clear path for me to sit down while she headed into the kitchen. With Sophie busying herself in the other room I sat down in the slice of light that came in from there, popping open the beer and pouring myself a shot before my butt had settled onto the cushion. Returning, Sophie clucked in what I thought was disapproval, at first I assumed because of the drinking. But then she flipped on the living room lights and I saw she had held a bottle of wine. She moved around the outside of the table and sat down again, giving me a smile that I supposed was meant to set me at ease, but didn't.

Sophie poured herself some wine into an Old Fashioned glass and that was just white trash enough to make me comfortable in a way that her smile didn't. I picked up my own glass and gestured it to her. She raised hers and we toasted to God-knows-what and we drank.

I shook off the burn and blinked the water out of my eyes. Staring straight ahead the black box of the television's screen loomed and for the first time during this entire Italian escapade I wished the TV were on. I picked up the beer and sipped on it, the cool liquid washing the burn of the liquor away, and tried to think of something to say.

"Marine?" Sophie's accent made the word so

One Sore Rib

unfamiliar I didn't recognize it at first. When I did I felt a passing annoyance – Cheryl had been talking to Sophie about me but not to Sophie about herself. That had always been a sore spot between us, her willingness to share things about me that I wasn't sure I wanted shared. But it had been one of those things that it was either learn to let it go and love her, or to let her go.

"Yeah."

"Ha fatto combattere nella guerra?"

I didn't know what she was asking, but I knew the word for war in nine languages. Whenever people asked about this sort of thing they always asked the same questions anyway.

"Yeah," I repeated. I set the Peroni down on the table and held the imaginary barrel of a rifle with my left hand while holding its grip in my right, moving the whole non-existent system in a shaking motion like a 10-year-old boy simulating recoil. "Marine."

Sophie pulled her knees to her on the couch, concern bunching up around her eyes. I couldn't tell if she was worried for me or if this new information had changed her opinion of me. It was usually one or the other. I went back to my drink, pouring myself another shot, comfortable with the silence now that it had a familiar cause. I had gotten used to that too, I guess.

"Che cosa si desidera fare dopo la guerra?" I looked over at Sophie, a bit surprised to see her expression had changed. The accustomed expressions of sympathy for my experiences, or fake awe at my service, or muted revulsion at my imagined crimes against humanity weren't there in her face. Instead there was the same kind of honest, curious happiness I had seen in her face at her first meeting Cheryl.

I had no idea what to say. "What?"

"Dopo," she made a gesture with her eyes as if tracking something moving in a parabolic arc above her head. She accompanied the next word with her own imitation of my air rifle, "La guerra." She dropped her hands, making the rifle disappear, gazing at me questioningly.

After the war. I hadn't thought about that in a long time and hadn't been asked about it in an even longer span. It felt like I had just gotten home soil under my feet when the Beast and his Master had pulled the carpet out from under us. I went back to my beer, sipping on it, not sure how to answer that. Eventually, tired and unsure, I just shrugged. "I don't know."

Sophie's eyes narrowed, clearly doubting the answer I wasn't sure she understood. She let a moment pass to give me a second chance at a reply. I didn't answer, though, until she reached out with one of her long legs and poked me in the shoulder with her big toe.

"I don't know," I shrugged, trying to appear as honest as I felt. "I mean, I used to know exactly what I wanted." I paused, thinking about what I'd just said, the admission of it causing me pain. It grew in my chest until I couldn't hold onto it. The whole answer came out in a torrent that couldn't possibly be understood by Sophie with her rudimentary grasp of English, but I just kept going anyway.

"I knew exactly what I wanted." Despite the discomfort of it, I smiled at the memory as it crystallized. My smile grew, happy to talk about a happy bit of the past. "I remember at Thanksgiving in like '99 or sometime before the whole world went nuts, Cheryl and I were on the outs. We did that a lot – broke up, got back together, broke up." I marked each inversion of the relationship roller coaster with a nod of my head and Sophie nodded too as if she understood. "But this time was different because I think we both knew that we wanted each other more than anything else. But we fought anyway that year, in front of our parents and friends and God and everybody and she asked me what I wanted. And I told her."

I paused and took a serious pull from the beer, trying to dull the pain caused by the nostalgia and the happiness and the cutting edge of a too-clear memory. "I told her I wanted to be a Marine, I wanted to marry her, for us to have kids, and for us raise them Catholic."

And there I was holding that in my hand when I realized why I hadn't wanted to pick it up. "But here is it ten years later and my wife is dying, the children never came, and as much as I always wanted to I don't think I ever believed in Jesus." I tried to hold back the tears that were pushing out of me but I couldn't quite manage it. So I took another drink.

"I'm sorry," I said wiping my eyes, "I'm gonna go to bed." I tried not to look at Sophie. I was suddenly very tired in my bones and behind my eyes. I thought about all the things that I had wanted to ask Sophie, about the Old Man and the Kid, about whether Verdicchio was a real thing, about how she got here, and a bunch of other things that had been really very important just a few hours ago. But now I was too tired to care. I got up and headed to the stairs.

"Mi è piaciuto quello che ho visto quando ti ho visto nuda," Sophie spoke softly from behind me. I turned back to her. Still on the couch, she was peaking over the back lip of it, her expression that of someone trying to say or do something nice for a stranger they suddenly and inexplicably cared about. I could see by the amusement of her smile that puzzlement was all over my face. But there was something else there, a happiness in the freedom to say what she wanted without consequence, safe in the knowledge that I couldn't understand one word out of that sentence, more or less determine its meaning.

"Sure thing," I said.

Sophie smiled, finished her drink in one go, then stood up. She moved towards me, stepping between me and the stairs, bringing her close enough that she stopped on her way by me. Bending at the waist she gave me a kiss on the cheek, still wearing that bemused smile. The kiss lingered just long enough to leave a warmth that made me feel there might be something more to it than affection or kindness. Opening my eyes without realizing I'd closed them, I saw she was blushing. That vision produced in me an insane moment where in my mind's eye I crushed her to me, getting to feel the body I had been thinking about in my most weak or bored moments. I kissed her, and kept kissing her, a real kiss, a kiss between a man and woman and something I hadn't had in a very long time.

The deepening blush on her cheeks told me that my thoughts must have been clear. The notion that I was that transparent caused my own cheeks to redden. Then she ducked her eyes away from mine, went upstairs and left me alone.

I shouldn't have, but the next day after I woke up, I felt better, cleaner and lighter somehow. For the first time in awhile I stepped out of the apartment with a spring in my step. The gremlin on my shoulder was back telling me that I should feel sick with guilt, but I just put it aside and kept on walking.

While they didn't help communicate with Sophie, our topics too complex and intimate for rudimentary skill, the last days' language lessons did help with the

One Sore Rib

grocery list. I did fumble my speech on an item or two though, causing the old fruit merchant to take the list from me.

He nodded his head as he read down it, clearly approving. He smiled and made a joke about the list that I didn't get but I smiled and laughed seeing the humor through his even-in-the-rain sunglasses. I didn't understand his next question either, so I shook my head and shrugged my shoulders in one motion, the universal symbol for "Non so lo." At least I had become fluent in that bit of Italian.

The old merchant replied in the same language by motioning out the hourglass figure of a woman in front of him with his hands. He finished it out with a thrust of his hips for good measure, adding, "You have a woman now, yes?"

The crudity of the gesture and his first use of English to me in anything other than prices surprised me, making me laugh out loud. For the lack of a clear or easy answer I just nodded my head and said, "Yes." This made the old merchant smile and he gave me a free orange with my purchases and sent me on my way.

The day was wet and gray and the cold clung to the stone walls of the apartment stairwell, but the old merchant's joke kept me laughing until I was coming up on the second floor. Like a swimmer rising out of the water, moving above the lip of the second stairwell changed the pressure around me. I wasn't sure why, but I slowed my pace, lightly putting each footfall on the stair above the other until I saw the door to Sophie's old place.

I stood there for a moment as my body and mind went rigid, a tunnel forming around my vision to the door. The open door. It was barely ajar, but hadn't clicked shut whenever the last person had gone through it. I waited, listening, but didn't hear any noise coming from inside. After what felt like a very long time I set down the grocery bags on the stairhead and walked to the door. I pushed it open with my palm, feeling every divot and feature as my hand slid across its surface.

The apartment had been tossed. I imagined a squad of Italianos going through and clearing bookcases with the ends of their rifles, tossing up furniture, smashing walls in frustration. I went through every room, finding the same level of confounded destruction in each one.

"They didn't find anything," I said to the empty room. "They don't know where she is."

I went back out and picked up the groceries and whistled my way up the final flight of stairs.

Chapter 12

All of that lasted until an afternoon when there was knock on the door.

On that day I'd returned from morning errands to find Sophie was already in the kitchen. She was singing lightly to herself as she went about making breakfast. I could smell coffee brewing and started to head in to get a cup. Then I thought about that blush that seemed to be coming into Sophie's cheeks more often. That worried me as much as I enjoyed it. I decided to head upstairs instead.

The familiar jangle of the wire balusters started as I hit the first steps, but I stopped when I heard, "Where ya goin'?" from the couch.

I stopped, turning on the third stair, and stepped back down to walk over to the couch. Lying in her usual spot was my wife, smiling weakly up at me, clearly enjoying my surprise. "Hi."

"Hi," I echoed her greeting back to her, as was our custom. "How'd you...?" My eyes asked the rest of the question, moving between the couch and stairs and back again.

"Sophie and I managed." Her weak smile grew brighter with a bit of pride.

I bent down and kissed her saying, "Good for you," not really sure how I felt about it. "I'll be right back. I'm gonna put away the groceries and make you breakfast."

The smile disappeared as sallow distaste at the idea of eating rolled down Cheryl's face. "I'm not so sure that last bit's a good idea."

I tried to hide my worry with a look of sympathy, rubbing her arm gently with my palm. "Give it a shot and see how it goes," I suggested. She nodded, anxiety deepening in her features. I kissed her again, letting it linger a bit longer than the first one.

Moving into the kitchen with the groceries Sophie turned from the tiny stove and gave me a smile as well. Putting the bags on the counter next to her I began to unload them, soliciting the occasional murmur of approval as particular items came out. Taking out a zucchini her murmur became louder by several decibels and went up a few octaves, a happy reaction that I couldn't help but smile at. Her eyes went from the zucchini to my eyes and she could clearly see the amusement on my face. Holding out the phallic-looking vegetable I couldn't keep an eyebrow from arching and a smirk off my lips as I held it and said, "You want this?"

Whether the intention of my phrase was clear or Sophie had gotten far enough along in her English lessons for this to make sense, she blushed and snorted lightly as she held back a laugh. The snort, an unladylike noise if there ever was one, converted my own smirk into a full-fledged smile. She snatched the zucchini out of my hand and smacked me on the shoulder with it. Then, still grinning, she went back to the stove. I kept smiling through the rest of the grocery unloading. It had been hard at first not to linger on the ghosts of the visitors to her apartment, but I tried to push it to the back of my mind and just enjoy what I could of the morning.

As predicted, Cheryl hardly touched her breakfast. By the time I came out of the kitchen she was staring at the television as if wishing it on, but hadn't touched the remote, which was just a few inches from her on the coffee table. I bent forward, giving her a kiss on the forehead as I put the slurry into her hands. She took it, but just continued to stare at the TV, not really registering the kiss or the food. Moving back to sit at her feet, I pulled on her big toe, "Eat up." I tried to sound encouraging.

"Ernh," was her only reply as she put the straw from the cup to her lips but didn't actually suck on it. "Here," I said, as if offering help, and picked up her right foot and began to massage the sole of it with my thumbs, pushing into the now barely-there flesh, trying to coax something out of her other than the blank stare at the TV. It felt like rubbing a bundle of sticks.

A curling of her toes and a rolling back of her head combined with a quiet groan told me that my administrations were helping, or at least giving Cheryl some pleasure. That was all the encouragement I needed to keep at it. Either as a reward for my efforts or out of a sense of gratitude she tried a few sips of her breakfast. After a short time, though, she set the slurry down on the table and fell asleep as I rubbed. I set her foot down, picked up the slurry, said "Good enough," and took it into the kitchen.

Out of idle curiosity I sucked on the slurry as I walked back into the kitchen and made quite a face as I puckered, if the laugh that came from Sophie was any indication. I looked over at her as she chortled and saw she had set out two places on the tiny kitchen table. With a murmur of thanks I sat down to breakfast. It smelled wonderful and with Sophie sitting across from me the view was great, but I just picked at the food, casting frequent glances out to Cheryl to see if she was still asleep. Sophie absent-mindedly tapped her fork against the plate in front of her, gazing into the morning light that was filtering through the south window.

For some reason then I thought about my father and his own interminable end and how my mother had sounded when she called me the morning he had died. She hadn't sounded relieved, but there certainly wasn't any surprise, and I remember her voice sounding dry, tired, and used up. After awhile the waiting had become its own very long funeral, heavy and plodding, eventually even the suffering and sadness inside of you calling for it to end.

At least the television wasn't on.

That thought gave me a black chuckle, eliciting a quizzical look from Sophie. I grinned back at her and suddenly found my appetite had returned and I dug into my food. While it may have appeared as a standard issue bacon sandwich, I tasted strong pepper, tomato, spinach, cheese, and other good things I couldn't place. The change in my enthusiasm pleased Sophie who smiled and began to fork pieces of egg into her mouth.

We sat like that, eating, trying to enjoy a little piece of Italian sunshine, trying not to think about the dying woman in the other room. But then my blood ran cold when Cheryl cried out in a plaintive way that I hadn't heard before. I jumped up and ran into the living room where she was wrestling with the blankets on her, trying to get out of them and off the couch.

"Hey, hey," I said as gently as I could, trying not to let my own fear into my voice. "Where ya goin'?"

Her eyes shot open, marbled with red veins and madness, but then they focused and recognized me. "I ... uh ..." she stuttered a moment, coming back from wherever she had been, "I thought you were gone."

"Nope," I gave her the best smile I could muster and ran my hand over her scalp. It came away wet with a sweat that smelled of something that wasn't quite my wife. "Not going anywhere."

"Good," she said softly. Whatever demon of panic that had nearly lifted her off the couch left her as she settled back into its soft depths. After a few moments of gently caressing her eyes fluttered again, coming to a rest, but not quite closed.

"Hey, how about we go up to the roof?" I asked as I continued to run my hand along her head. Without quite opening her eyes she gave me her usual wistful smile and said, "That'd be nice."

I picked up the lingering nothing of Cheryl's weight and hoofed up the two flights to the terrace. The plants were still wet from the morning dew but the sun was out, so I set her down on a bench, sitting behind her to bolster her up so she could watch Venice wake up if she wanted. I did just that, staring out at the jutting orange and yellow of the Venetian rooftops and smelled the ocean air and smiled to myself. "It's nice out today," I said.

Cheryl just gave a happy groan as if I were trying to wake her from a too-good sleep and burrowed back against me. I craned my head down to kiss the top of her head.

Sophie came up a few moments later. She walked over to bend down and check on Cheryl. Satisfied with whatever mystery inspection she had conducted, she brushed her hair out of her eyes, gave me a smile, stood up straight, then walked to the terrace's southern end and stood at the wooden railing, viewing the city with a disinterest only possible by a native. An evil, inexplicable thought came to me then, to push Sophie off the terrace, down the three stories to the cobblestone streets below. The image of her broken, crushed body bleeding out in the alley below came into my mind so suddenly and clearly I looked away from her and couldn't look back.

I was wrestling with that when I found myself wrestling with Cheryl in a very real way. Her arms and legs shot out, pushing her against me with surprising force and kicking off most of the blankets. As she thrashed, she let out a series of meaningless whooping sounds. I wrapped my arms around her, restraining her and keeping her on the bench. Sophie flew over and sat on the remainder of blankets, pinning her feet. After half a minute of panic, the madness passed as quickly as it had come and Cheryl collapsed into my arms, not unconscious but not quite awake.

I could feel alarm stampede through me. I glanced at Sophie and to see the same dismay in her eyes. Unable to provide any explanation or comfort to anyone on that rooftop I held Cheryl closer, holding her head to my cheek and tried to get a bearing.

I let long enough pass till I felt like there wasn't going to be an encore, then gestured for Sophie to come over and take Cheryl from me. She held her by the shoulders while I slipped out from behind Cheryl, then Sophie took my place. I whispered something about pain pills and, to my surprise, planted a kiss on top of Sophie's head. I stood there, bent at the waist, wondering at what I'd just done, then scuttled to the top of the stairs before I had to explain myself to Sophie.

In the kitchen I raided the last bottle of pills in the pantry, shaking it as if doing so would magically cause the bottle to produce more. I counted out the paltry number while thinking about the remaining cash on hand and tried to remember if there were any credit cards that weren't maxed out.

My mental math was interrupted by a knock on the door. I felt my eyes pop open and my heart momentarily stop, then begin to race. I surveyed the kitchen, half-expecting someone to be standing behind me. No one there, the kitchen filled with another knock from the door. I gripped my dread by its neck and listened to the knock with all the rationality I could muster: It was a soft knock, not some monster bash like I would have used, a polite rap, something that might be used by visiting neighbor. Crossing the living room I tried to banish the images of the Old Man and the Kid. I peered through the peephole, then opened the door.

Dennis was standing there, wearing his always taciturn expression. Combined with his permanent tan and the deep lines on his face he could have passed for a cigar store Indian. I leaned with my arm up against the doorframe, looking down at him for a long moment. Neither of us seemed happy to see the other.

"Howdy."

"Hi."

"Surprised to see me?" Dennis asked.

I thought about that. "No," I replied. "It actually explains a lot."

"Well then," he said, stepping aside from the door, "let's go see the man."

"Give me a minute." I didn't invite him in, but closed the door. I headed up the stairs until I was sure he couldn't hear me through the thick door then I rushed up to the rooftop garden, taking the final steps three at a time.

I found Sophie and Cheryl resting right where I had left them, still peaceful. Seeing both of them I felt my chest go tight with the uncertainties in front of me: I couldn't help but think about Cheryl waking up without me or if Sophie could physically handle a dementia episode on her own. But to refuse Dennis' ostensibly polite request felt somehow more dangerous than going with him. His arrival filled me with the same desire as having a live hand grenade land in my lap – I wanted to get it as far away from me and mine as possible.

One Sore Rib

I handed a confused Sophie the pain pills and jangled the house keys in front of her, letting her know I had them and trying to tell her not to let anyone in while I was gone. The confusion on her face contracted into concern, but she just nodded and pulled Cheryl closer to her. Fairly certain she understood, I headed downstairs.

"Let's go," I said, stifling an impulse to apologize for taking so long. I closed the door behind me without making a show of the keys, knowing it would lock automatically. Dennis stuffed his hands into the pockets of the green windbreaker he was wearing and headed to the stairs without waiting to see if I'd follow.

I did, trailing him down the stone steps and out the front door. We headed north in the alley and I fell in beside him as he pushed into the crowd at a T-junction. While Dennis navigated the narrow streets with the same kind of easy confidence that Sophie had, I quickly became lost in the maze of the sestiere. Neither of us said anything for a time.

A few more turns and Dennis had taken us away from the tourists through empty back streets. Even with the crowds gone, the claustrophobia of street-level Venice didn't die – its walls jumped straight up and pushed in, giving the light only one direction to rain down from. But it gave me a sense of security that we were alone as there was nowhere for anyone to hide. Walking under a sotoportego I found myself possessed by a negative impulse and I aired it by saying, "They didn't know where she was."

Dennis paid more attention to the architecture around us than what I had to say, gazing absently up and around at it. Without taking his eyes from it he replied, "They knew she couldn't have gone far."

"You mean they knew because you told them."

He snapped on his heels then, pivoting to me so quickly I stepped back half-expecting a punch in the face when he pulled his hand from his pocket. Instead he pointed a finger at me saying, "I didn't ask you to bring your troubles here. And I told you to stay away from the girl – advice you ignored."

He finished with, "Don't try to lay this on me," and went back to walking. I followed, trying not to let my sullenness at his betrayal make me feel like a child being pulled in by the authority of an adult. I let my mind wander to what kind of ambush I might be walking into as I went along the canals with him.

Eventually Dennis led me to a piazza, far from the Grand Canal, with brown segmented squares marking out the ground and white buildings for its walls. One of the buildings had claimed part of the square as its own with an outdoor espresso bar. Small sandalwood tables sat on the terrace, umbrellas sprouting from the middle of each to hide the chairs around them from the noon sun. Sitting at one of the tables was a thin older man wearing a Borsalino straw hat, a white button-down shirt, and white linen slacks. He sat with his legs crossed, reading a paper and drinking from an espresso cup. He looked like he had been sitting there waiting forever and would continue to sit there long after I was gone.

"There he is," Dennis said from his temporarily forgotten position at my side. I nodded and walked into the square.

It was so empty of life that I felt my paranoia sit up as I made my way over to the table. I scanned the area, but the square was small with nowhere to hide. Other than the man in white the only other person was a teenager behind the counter. Despite the ill-fitting tuxedo he wore, he didn't look like he worked there. He pulled uncomfortably at his starched collar

One Sore Rib

and didn't say a thing to me as I got closer. I had seen his expression on other young men. He was examining me for threat detection.

His hatchet face and oily skin didn't make him more appealing. The huge espresso machine behind him had more character – the dents on its chrome body promised a storied past, probably involving looting in the last world war. The mysterious appendages sprouting off of it reminded me of a dentist's office for some reason I couldn't fathom, but I found disconcerting nonetheless.

I walked over to the older man. He didn't raise his eyes to me until my shadow fell on him. "Verdicchio."

He smiled, which I didn't expect, his grizzled hair poking out from under his hat, his hawk nose nearly sticking out beyond its rim. The smile touched his dark eyes, his eyebrows lifting, making it appear earnest. This made me distrust him instantly.

"Buongiorno," he said, pushing a chair out from the table towards me with an expensive looking leather shoe. "You are Dennis' American, non?"

"Yeah." I felt the answer pull the corners of my mouth down at being described that way.

"Good, good," he extended a hand to shake mine. "I am Felice Verdicchio." He smiled again adding, "But you already knew that."

I took his hand, gave it a firm shake and introduced myself. He asked me to and I sat down, putting us a little closer together than I was comfortable with. He set aside his copy of *la Repubblica*, flattening out the sports section on the table with both hands. "Can you believe these cazzos?" he asked, indicating a team I was unfamiliar with on the page. I shrugged, giving a pretty good impression that I didn't care about the team or whatever his stake in it was. He made a gesture, slapping the offending paper away saying, "Balenas."

He turned his full attention to me then and asked, "Would you like something to eat? Something to drink?" I shook my head and said, "I'm good," and almost immediately regretted it. Having something in front of me could have been useful and Verdicchio didn't give the impression he was in a hurry. I doubt he ever did.

"I hope coming here wasn't too much of an inconvenience."

"Not at all," I lied. "Dennis knocked on our door just as me and my wife were finishing breakfast."

"Ah, yes, your wife," Verdicchio's face became covered with something that might have been concern. "Dennis has mentioned her as well. I'm sorry she is not well."

"Thank you." I felt myself relax a little as I let that familiar falsehood out. I had dealt with so many disingenuous sympathies about Cheryl by now that handling one, even from a potentially dangerous unknown like Verdicchio, was old hat.

"But I'm sure you are in a hurry to get back to her."

"Not at all. She'll be fine until I return." That stuck a bit, feeling like a sharp pill fragment caught in my throat. Verdicchio sensed this, his smile growing a bit by a short reptilian length.

"Then you must be in a hurry for other reasons. You Americans are always in a hurry."

Another shrug, an attempt to regain my composure of indifference. "I suppose."

"Dennis has told me that you are not the average American though. I must say from what little I know, I must agree."

"Thanks?" I made sure the inflection in my voice carried the question mark. He laughed at that, which told me his grasp of English was more than a little fluent, a piece of information I pocketed for future reference.

"It is true," he said, taking off his hat and mopping the top of his head, bald beneath from forehead to crown. As the day continued it was getting warmer in the small square. "Most Americans would have scuttled back to their cruise ships if Franco and Carlo had so much as waggled a finger at them."

"Who?" I knew he meant the Old Man and the Kid, but I asked anyway.

"Franco and Carlo," Verdicchio replied, unperturbed by my fake ignorance. "The two men you met in your apartment building."

"Your men?"

He nodded, lips pursed, not saying anything.

"They were making a lot of noise," I offered in the way of an explanation.

"Yes, please forgive them. They often get overly excited in their duties."

"And what, exactly, are their duties?"

"Why, to protect Sophie, of course," he said, leaning back in his chair, eyes a little wider, like it was the most obvious thing in the world. I sat on that for a second, trying to keep the disbelief off my face.

I went with as neutral a question as I could think of. "Protect her from what?"

"Mio giovane," he said, leaning back in his chair, somehow adopting both a fatherly and worldly air at the same time, "I have been doing business in Veneto for more than four decades. I have seen our local industries go from shoe repair and buttons to industrial waste disposal and model gondolas. And I have been involved in all of them, trying to protect the people of *La Serenissima* the entire time. Some people," he leaned forward at this, his voice lowering to a conspiratorial tone, "do not appreciate this."

It came off as more than a little condescending and I can't say that I liked it. "So she needs to be protected from you?" I asked, my tone coming out more pissy than I would have preferred.

"From my enemies, surely," he replied, his tone suggesting that my insinuation had hurt him.

"So what is she to you?"

"A daughter, a friend, a woman whose safety and company give me great comfort." He went through the alternatives, pausing between each, trying them out to see which one pleased me the most.

Unconvinced, I didn't say anything.

"Surely as a man who wishes to see his wife protected you can understand. Do you have children of your own?"

"No." For the first time I was grateful for that. The idea that a man like this was probably someone's grandfather reminded me that the predators in the world far outnumbered the protectors. And that sometimes they were one and the same.

"Then you cannot understand," he said and I nearly punched him in the face for it. I had long grown tired of people with children assuming that because I had none it somehow made me lesser than them or unable to understand the compassion and fear that came with being a parent. But before I could let my worse judgment get the better of me he continued with, "But you have some idea the feelings that Sophie inspire in me. So I ask your help."

"What?" I couldn't keep the surprise off my face. Out of all the ways I had seen this playing out this request wasn't one of them.

"I wish your help," he leaned back again, extending his palms to me as if begging me. "Your dispatching of Franco and Carlo then your disappearance of Sophie prove to me that she is much better in your care than in theirs."

"Also," he puffed out his cheeks in exasperation, "she does not like them." He crinkled his nose and shook his head as though he found the pair to be unsavory himself. "You cannot blame her. You have seen how they act."

"What about Dennis?" I asked quickly as an alternative. I felt like I was falling into a trap, outsmarted in a way that I couldn't quite understand.

Verdicchio shook his head again, his face only a few shades less unsettled by the idea than the alternative of the Old Man and the Kid. "Dennis has other duties," he said by way of explanation.

"As well, a man like you, in a foreign city with no friends, an ailing wife, with no property or means of income, surely you need some assistance yourself." He tilted his head with each item he listed off, stopping to stare at me as he finished.

I felt the trap shut on me with the promise of money. The empty pain-killer bottles, the maxed out credit cards, the lease running out on the apartment, all piled up behind me to give a mighty push right into it.

"Besides," he added with a casualness that only made it that much more ominous, "your friend Castardi assures me you can be trusted."

I stumbled for words, but nothing coherent came out. My mind boggled at the idea that Verdicchio had the kind of reach his statement implied.

"I don't ask much," he said, taking my bumbling as protest, "just that you keep doing as you are. Watch her, keep her safe. And I will see that you are compensated for your time and trouble."

"You were a soldier, yes?" The sudden change in subject jostled my confused mind even more resulting in a nod and a muttered, "Yeah," from me.

He clapped his hands together and smiled brightly as though this news gave him the greatest joy he had ever known. "See? You are perfect for this."

"When I was a young man," Verdicchio slid his eyes to the young man behind the counter, leaving me with the impression that he didn't want him to hear, "I joined the Foreign Legion and went to many far away lands." He drew back from me then, spreading his hands out, the smile on his face indicating how foolish he was in his youth, "I was seeking adventure."

Sitting forward again he whispered to me in a conspiratorial tone, "I hope you know that adventure is no place to take a sick wife."

The idea struck me as so ridiculous that it was all I could do to keep a straight face. "I'm not looking for adventure."

"Then why are you here?"

I thought about Cheryl and her wish to be here and decided it was none of his damn business. "No point really."

"Surely, you must have a reason."

"Sir," I found my voice again, finding certainty in what I was saying as I was saying it, "I'm an American at the beginning of the 21st century. I define pointless." I emphasized the word 'define' like I was proud of it, even though I wasn't.

He laughed, but I could see in his eyes that he didn't understand. He put an elbow of one arm on the table, the other bent to point at me, all rakish smile and easy demeanor. "But you have found a point, yes? In our Sophie?"

I shrugged, unsure of myself again, and muttered something in the affirmative.

"Then do this. Do this for Sophie." His brown eyes had an urgency then that made it feel suddenly like I had no choice. "Do this for me, and I will see you are rewarded."

So I said, "Okay."

The urgency drained out of his dark eyes to be replaced with a relieved happiness as he smiled again. "Good, good." He gestured to the boy behind the counter, "You must have a drink with me."

I heard Cheryl's voice in my head chiding me for drinking before lunch, again, but I said, "Yeah, sure." The boy brought over two glasses; small, tall glasses with no stems, each carrying a fair quantity of a yellow liquid I didn't recognize. Verdicchio held up his glass to me and said, "Cin-cin," and we both drank it down. It was a bittersweet taste that burned.

"I should go," I said after a few seconds of pretending to appreciate it. "Get back to the job you're paying me for."

"Good, good," Verdicchio said again. "Do not leave her alone for long."

I got up as the boy returned again, this time with an espresso. Standing, it occurred to me to ask, "What if I need to speak with you?"

Blowing gently on his coffee he said over it, "You know where to find Dennis. You may speak with him."

I looked down at him then, not sure how to process that information, but feeling as if it changed the relationship somehow. Not sure how to react or how to extricate myself from this particular social situation I just nodded and turned to leave.

As I was walking out of the square, I passed by Dennis who was leaning against the wall of the alley we had come in from. He slowed my march by reaching into his jacket and pulling out a thin but padded envelope and handing it to me. I took it and kept walking, but stopped when I realized it was money. Looking inside there was a sizable bunch of

Euros in various denominations.

Without taking my eyes off the envelope I asked, "How did he know I'd say yes?"

Dennis didn't answer. I looked his way to find him smiling that thin, unhappy smile of his. He grinned at me and said, "He always knows." He turned and walked away with a, "G'day, mate."

I watched him go with a mix of anger and disappointment. The anger was easy to put aside. Dennis' situation didn't seem that different from my own – a stranger in a strange land, now dependent on an odd and inscrutable master. I couldn't be angry at him for something that I might have done myself. The disappointment was harder to put aside. He was compromised now, just another piece of the alien Venetian landscape. Now where was I going to drink?

Chapter 13

Arriving back at the apartment the women were waiting for me. Sophie was roaming between the two windows in the living room, holding her hands like she wished she had a cigarette. Cheryl was, of course, on the couch, hidden from my place at the door. She revealed herself to me by angrily asking, "Where have you been?"

I walked over, trying to restrain the hope that the envelope full of currency had been attempting to etch into my chest the entire march back. I bent over the back of the couch and kissed Cheryl on the forehead, but her scowl told me that a smile and kiss weren't going to get me out of this one. Moving around to the other side of the couch I parked myself on the armrest as I said, "Dennis dropped by to see me." I was aware that Sophie was glaring at me with the same type of hostile concern as Cheryl, only restrained from giving voice to this by the language barrier.

At my answer Cheryl examined me suspiciously. "You don't smell like you've been drinking."

I resisted the urge to point out that lately Cheryl couldn't smell alcohol on me if I had been swimming in it. Instead I said, "We didn't go to the bar. He had someone he wanted me to meet."

"Who?" I could feel Sophie staring at me as well, both women's eyes on me causing my temperature to rise. I struggled under that heat on how to explain that I had known about Verdicchio from the beginning, that he was potentially dangerous, how I had gotten involved with Sophie because of some misguided ideas about using that connection to make money. And how it had, on the face of it, worked in the end but instead of me using Sophie, Verdicchio was using me.

Trying to explain all that seemed suddenly very difficult and more self-incriminating than I liked. So I just said, "Verdicchio."

The heat in the room went cold as I kept my eyes on Cheryl's now confused face, trying not to look at Sophie as I felt feel her go rigid. "Who?"

Not able to resist the pull of Sophie's stare, I rotated off the couch to the chair between the two of them and regretted it instantly. I could only weather Sophie's expression of fear, suspicion, and betrayal for a few seconds before returning to Cheryl and saying, "Verdicchio. He's," I had to pause at the moment of description. What was Verdicchio? A father figure? A gangster? I didn't really know, so I went with what I did know. "He's the man that sent the people who were knocking on Sophie's door."

"The men she's afraid of?"

"The same," I continued, looking at Sophie to try and judge how much she was understanding the conversation. "He claims that they were here for her protection and that what happened was a..." Stop, pause, choose words carefully. "A misunderstanding."

"He sounds like your kind of guy." I know she only meant the creative but slightly less than forthcoming way I had originally described my encounter between the Old Man and the Kid (never to be Franco and Carlo in my mind). But the comparison hurt anyway.

Whether she saw that or not she asked, "Protection from who?"

"Maybe you should ask her."

"I'm asking you." Cheryl's hostility increased, as if the suggestion had touched on something taboo. Maybe I had – in the short time Sophie had been here Cheryl had demonstrated a willful ignorance towards her history.

"He says that he's got a lot of enemies and he cares about Sophie so his enemies might try to use her to hurt him." I found myself scratching my head in an attempt to avoid making eye contact with either of them.

When I raised my head Cheryl was staring a challenge at me. Even with bits of her wasting until it had started to rot her brain she could tell I wasn't telling the whole truth. She spoke in rapid Italian to Sophie, too fast for me to have a hope of following. Before I could figure out if that was intentional Sophie gave a short, sharp, bitter laugh and turned her back on me with a flip of her hair.

Watching Sophie with the same kind of probing stare she had just leveled at me, Cheryl said, "That doesn't sound like the whole story."

"Maybe not," I said, knowing full well that was the truth and knowing Cheryl knew it now too, "but my handling of his two men the other day left an impression. He wants to pay me to look after her."

Cheryl moved her gaze from Sophie to me with an incredulous raised eyebrow. "What are you, *Magnum P.I.*?"

"It'd be the same thing we've been doing but with one big difference." I took out the envelope of Euros and tossed them onto the blanket covering Cheryl's lap.

After investigating the contents of the envelope Cheryl, in a somewhat stunned tone, said, "That's a lot of money."

"Enough to pay for rent and pain pills for a few weeks." I couldn't help grin a little, feeling one of the impossible pressures of my life release a little. But it burned off my face in a hurry when Sophie noticed the envelope. She glared at it with such an expression of betrayal that it might have been made out of poison.

Cheryl glanced from the envelope to Sophie to me, her initial shock giving away to distrust and caution.

"What, exactly, would you be doing for this money?"

"The same thing we've been doing," I repeated, trying to sound reasonable, trying to keep desperation out of my voice. "She'll stay here with us and I'll keep anybody she doesn't want to see away."

Cheryl peered at me as she mentally picked through that sentence, trying to discern exactly what I meant. She turned to Sophie and spoke to her again in their exclusory language. Sophie's hostility appeared to ease into a kind of reserved hope when she replied with a question of her own.

Cheryl smiled, understanding and appreciation mixing together as she received Sophie's question. She returned to me and asked for both of them, "And what if the person she doesn't want to see is Verdicchio?"

I stopped trying to avoid Sophie's gaze as I thought about that. I could see miles of problems coming out of the implied suggestion and every one of them probably showed on my face. But I said to her, "He's asked me to protect you. He wasn't real particular about what I protected you from."

Cheryl smiled, pretty pleased with that answer, almost proud of me in a strange whimsical way, and passed it on to Sophie. Sophie smiled and nearly hopped a bit as she digested what we had said to her. I half-expected her to give a little clap but instead she jumped forward and gave me a kiss on the cheek and then bent down to kiss Cheryl as well. With that she ran up the stairs, so light that she didn't even rattle the wires on the spiral staircase.

"Where's she going?" I asked, for some ridiculous reason imagining her changing into lingerie.

"I don't know," Cheryl said, leaning back into her blankets and pillows on the couch. "But I think she's happy."

Chapter 14

And so was I, I suppose. Or as close as I could be for a few days. Cheryl didn't have any new dementia episodes so I could pretend that she was just ill, that maybe this story would have a different ending than all the stories that came before it. She slept for most of the time not even bothering to torture me with Italian television. I spent most of my time hovering over her, with concern in my mouth and in my eyes. And if I couldn't stand that anymore, I stepped outside to run errands, some of which were pretty flimsy excuses for errands. But when I left the house I did it with a fistful of Euros, which always made me feel better. I still kept an eye out for the Old Man and the Kid, or any other suspicious characters. I also changed the locks and showed Sophie how to brace the door from the inside.

On most days coming back from the pharmacy or the market I'd take a circuitous return route, telling myself I was watching to see if someone was tailing me. One thing I will say for Venice – it's a terribly wonderful place to get lost in. Once you lose sight of the ocean it's tight and narrow enough that getting disoriented is incredibly easy and you find yourself not knowing where you are before you know it. And there's something to see around every corner: An ancient church built by some forgotten family of merchants in the hopes of securing some small piece of immortal glory through Christ; a tiny cafe run by someone trying to eke out a living in a changing world and difficult times; the grandeur of an opera house. Or you can just follow some murky canal that trails off into unknown mystery.

Until it doesn't. Eventually the channel would terminate at the Grand Canal or in the lagoon and whatever explorer fantasy I had been playing in my head would end with it. So I'd turn around and go home.

I couldn't see myself going down to the Mondiale. Although thinking of Dennis came with a pang of betrayal, there was a part of me that still wanted to go down to the bar and pull up a stool and ask him how he was doing. There was something about him that had seemed trapped before. Learning more about Verdicchio had only marked this more clearly. And, for some reason I couldn't quite identify, that made me want to see him all the more. But giving up Dennis and the comforts of a familiar bar were small exchanges for what we had now.

Most of the time. As Cheryl continued to sleep more, I found myself frequently sitting on the couch with her laid out beside me, staring at the blank television. Time evaporated as it lingered indefinitely, each moment crystallizing into one long one, holding all potential and waiting to fall apart at a touch. And each moment would crack when Sophie sat down in one of the chairs catty-corner to the sofa and speak to me.

Most of the time I couldn't tell what she was saying. The first speech would usually snap me out of the torpor and I'd move my eyes to focus on her. Once I was there again she'd usually try to speak to me, either to ask a question or make a statement, in the little English she knew, sometimes trying to coax some Italian out of me.

But I'd eventually find myself just staring at her mouth, watching it move in a way that was untouched by wounds, disease, or old age. I'd listen to her talking, grateful for the noise, but rather than respond my eyes would start to move across her. Going from her hair to her eyes, down her increasingly heavy clothes as Venice marched into November, I began to understand why Verdicchio wanted Sophie. I couldn't quite parse out if Sophie held something that I wanted because I used to possess it, I never had it, or it just wasn't mine. But I couldn't avoid the unenviable conclusion that me and Verdicchio had something in common, whether I liked it or not. That realization mixed shame in with my sorrow and, though I loved her a bit for just trying to reach out to me, I'd usually turn away and there would be two zombies on the couch.

As much as I somnambulated through the days I suppose it shouldn't be surprising I wasn't sleeping at night. If the days were brittle crystal the nights were an ocean, floating awake and on my back, from one moment to the next, gazing out at the stars through the slats of the window. If I did sleep there were times I'd wake up in the middle of the night and I'd be certain that Cheryl wasn't there anymore, she lay so still and heavy. In waking hours she felt so light, like she was just an apparition. In those nocturnal moments, though, she was as unmoving as any stone, as if one of those angels my mom was always on about had pinned her to the bed.

After I had verified that she was still breathing it was damned difficult to go back to sleep. So I'd kiss her gently as to not wake her, then hold her for awhile before rolling over and trying to sleep again.

On the nights that it was more impossible than hard, though, I'd get up and walk the perimeter of the apartment. Starting with the front door, I'd make sure that it was locked, although I knew it always was. From there I'd rotate into the kitchen, checking for silhouettes against the smoked glass, checking for rappellers or ninjas or whatever my brain had conjured up to worry about. In the living room, I'd peek through the curtains to the narrow streets below, half-expecting to see a trench-coated figure smoking under the white streetlamps. But there never was one.

Making my way back up the stairs as quietly as I could, I'd head to the end of the hall and out the glass doors, staring down at the street as I climbed up to the roof garden. Then, with all points clear, I'd spend some time staring out over the ancient skyline of Venice, trying to get the coppery taste of paranoia out of my mouth.

While it may have been beautiful during the daytime, at night the skyline of Venice's slanted and jutting rooftops were just a void of darkness, a chaotic mess as if someone had dumped so much junk on the island. As proud as they might be, I felt sorry for the Venetians then, stuck on their island, atop a withered empire that was slowly sinking into the ocean. It became clear that this was, as one post-deployment counselor had put it, the futility of trying to hold together an untenable situation.

Sitting on that roof, watching out for an enemy that wasn't there and probably wouldn't come, I realized I was hearing a lot of voices from my past lately. I wished one of them was my dad. Which is odd considering we hardly spoke while he was alive.

"Buonanotte," Sophie's quiet voice pulled me out of my poisoned nostalgia. She stood at the top of the stairs, waiting for permission to walk onto the terrace. Backlit by the white streetlamps from the alley below, her silhouette didn't leave a lot to the imagination, her tall, hour-glass figure eclipsing everything else around it. I blinked and went back to the ocean, not wanting to gawk, feeling my cheeks burn a little as embarrassment and desire mixed in me in a way that I hadn't felt in a long time. "Hi," I mumbled.

Taking that as permission, Sophie walked over, one foot in front of the other in a manner that would have been unremarkable any other time, but now the playfulness of it was unmistakable. Saying something in Italian, I could tell from her tone that she was smiling as she moved something from behind her back – a bottle that my expert eye could discern had already been opened and re-corked.

I got up. Despite the recent hours of stupor I did so with an urgency that was buzzing in my head, telling me to get out. The claustrophobia was back, but in a way that made me want to run instead of making me feel trapped.

Sophie stopped me with a hand on my chest. I brushed it off, but it found its way back again with a speed that made me look her in the eye.

What I found there stopped me. It wasn't lust or pity or playfulness, but a confusion that was touched with a calm concern. It had a gentleness that kept me from moving her hand again. She whispered something then and gently pushed on my chest until the back of my knees hit the bench and I sat down, Sophie whispering something that I couldn't understand.

I averted my eyes as I felt her fingers move through my hair, trying to hide the heat that felt like it was going to burn through my skin. Through the nightgown she was wearing her figure made me think of the valleys and softness of Cheryl's body before the operations and chemotherapy.

That conflict was too much, the thoughts of Sophie too much. I had to move my eyes up to hers, the simple softness of her navel having too strong a pull.

Feeling ashamed and weak and conflicted, I raised

One Sore Rib

my chin so she could see, unflinchingly, the mess I was. Her fingers brushed against my forehead and she said softly, "Poverino."

Something moved out of me then and I could feel the tears well up. Not even the shame I felt I should feel was enough to stop them. When they came in earnest it wasn't with any sort of dignity, but with great sobbing hiccups that sounded like a child, a baby, someone crying beyond control or reproach. Sophie didn't say anything then, just wrapped her arms around my head, bringing my face to her belly, tears staining her nightgown. She held me like that until I stopped crying, and in that cold October evening, I cried for a very, very long time.

Chapter 15

When I woke up the sky was beginning to turn blue with the sun and my toes blue from the cold. Rising in the beginning of that bleak light my eyelids felt sticky, my head thick, and my body sore. I groaned as I pushed myself up from the wooden plank I had fallen asleep on. Rolling up onto my haunches a blanket that hadn't been there before fell off of me. I pulled it back to me as a breeze blew off the ocean and skimmed across the exposed terrace. Even feeling like my eyes had been glued shut the cold wind caused them to open and for me to sit upright.

    Putting my feet onto the deck, still slick with dew and that much colder for it, I suddenly found myself very awake, if still sore with fatigue. I shivered and was grateful for the blanket. Pulling it tighter around my shoulders, I wondered how it got there, thought of Sophie and smiled, grateful and without shame, which felt inexplicable to me. But it made me smile all the same.

    After a few moments of mentally going over the inventory of all of my parts I was satisfied everything was there. I waddled over to the terrace railing where the sun on my left providing some much needed warmth. In the early light of dawn Venice had been returned to its beauty, with its slanting roofs and jutting towers, particularly gorgeous in the almost unnatural, delicate silence of the morning. Then I heard the blast of a cruise ship's horn and the noise of the boat traffic began to filter up from Saint Mark's Basin. I walked to the stairs causing a kit of pigeons to fly from a nearby roof and land on the railings around me, cooing for something to eat. Wrapped in the

One Sore Rib

blanket I waved them off with a feeble, if not unkind, hand and shuffled downstairs on feet so cold they felt like stumps.

I opened the glass doors as quietly as possible walking into the upstairs hall. Looking to my left and right I saw both Cheryl and Sophie were sound asleep in their own beds. I took a moment to check on Cheryl. She appeared comfortable and at peace, so I left her there with a kiss on the cheek. Stepping back into the hallway, I almost moved to the stairs, but instead headed into Sophie's room. I stood over her, wrapped in the blanket she had left me, and marveled at the mystery of her. After a brief hesitation I bent down and, out of appreciation or selfishness, kissed her on the forehead. Her eyelids fluttered, but then were still, and so I went downstairs.

I took some time to make myself coffee and then got about making Cheryl's breakfast slurry. The sound of the blender miraculously didn't wake anyone so I set the cup down on the coffee table next to Cheryl's usual daytime resting place and made my way back upstairs. At the top I ran into Sophie, yawning and pushing a hand through her disheveled hair as she came out of her room. I smiled at her, part affection and part amusement, and she smiled at me with sleepy eyes through loose hair. I was surprised to find myself smiling without embarrassment. As she passed me I took her hand between my thumb and forefinger in the smallest gesture of affection, tugging on it as I whispered, "Thanks."

Here eyes brightened and so did her smile with the soft reply of, "Non è niente." I let go of her hand. She went down the stairs and I went into our bedroom.

Cheryl lay on the bed, straight with hands by her side. It reminded me of too many people I'd seen on the cooling board so I walked right in and sat on the edge of the bed to run my palm over her bald head. Her eyes dully blinked and then scrunched together as if the sun coming in through the slatted window was causing her pain. I ran two fingers over the ridge of her skull, starting at her forehead, trying to push the pain out the back. "How're you doin'?" I asked.

"Hrm," came a not quite awake reply, "cold."

"Would you like a bath? Maybe that'd warm you up?"

She nodded feebly. I reached under the sheets to lift her, causing them to pull across her body as I took her off the bed. Even the thickness of the comforter couldn't hide that there wasn't much left of Cheryl or too much further to go. I ignored this and moved her into the bathroom.

After letting her do her business I lowered her into the bath and sat on the toilet to fiddle with the faucets, changing the temperature of the water to suit her. She seemed particularly finicky that morning.

"It's too hot," she said after the water had been running for only a few moments.

"OK, no problem," I yawned out and adjusted the ancient handles to produce colder water.

"That's too cold," Cheryl said, her tone carrying a rebuking quality.

"Warmer coming up."

"Are you trying to burn me?" came the question after only a few seconds of the new temperature.

"No, not at all." I stuck my wrist under the faucet to check the water and found it habitable for human conditions. Covering the handles with my hands I made turning motions, but didn't change anything.

"Too cold."

I stared at her with a smirk and a raised eyebrow. I kept doing that until she took her gaze away from the bathroom tiles to look at me, a low-level hostile suspicion clouding her expression. "What?"

"I hadn't changed anything Cheryl." It couldn't quite keep the gloating tone out of my voice, which didn't please her, but I only laughed when she weakly kicked water in my face.

"You seem like you're in a better mood today."

"Because I cracked the princess tub time code?" That response got me more water in the face. This time she laughed when I sputtered the water out of my mouth.

The water was high enough in the tub that Cheryl sank down so only the top of her head and nose broke the surface. I ran a bar of soap along the rest of her, up to my elbow in water. She watched me for awhile without saying a word. I smiled while cleaning her, the echo of her small laughter still in my head, happy that I had made her happy.

Then she surfaced to say, "It's OK to admit you like having her around."

Surprised, I covered it by pretending not to know what she was talking about. I think "Huh?" was my brilliant retort.

Idling just above the surface Cheryl pinned me with her stare. "Sophie. It's OK to admit you like her."

The raised eyebrow came back but this time with a faux-skeptical bent. "So you tell me to go get her, she stays, you spend hours talking to her in a language I don't understand, and she's here for my benefit?"

"That's not what I meant," rising to take the bait, water beading on her shoulders.

"Then I don't know what you're talking about."

Cheryl's gaze became harder. The fond memory of laughter drained out of the room as I flipped the lever, the plunger letting the water go. "Why is it always so hard for you to admit that you care about something?"

"Practice." I meant the answer to be flippant, but I could feel the hard edges around it as it left my mouth. A sure sign that I had, perhaps from the moment we met, started to care about Sophie and I didn't want to admit it. Cheryl sank down into the water, letting go of what had been her simmering anger. "It's still OK," she said quietly.

With that I found myself feeling very uncomfortable and I felt it in Cheryl too as I dried her off. I wrapped her in one of her sarongs from the bedroom, and carried her downstairs, all without so much as another word.

Sophie noises came from the kitchen with a cheerful, "Buongiorno," piping out as I laid Cheryl down on the couch. Cheryl at least tried to make as if she were going to eat, picking up her cup and chewing on the straw. I smiled at her as I pulled a blanket onto her, glad to see she had a little more energy today. I went so far as to suppress a groan as she reached for the remote. The cacophony of Italian television started up and I watched it dutifully with my wife for as long as I could stand, rubbing Cheryl's legs through the blanket. Eventually Cheryl dozed off and I got up to go into the kitchen. A knock on the door stopped me.

Unsure I had heard it, I took the remote and switched off the television. It came again – a short, sharp rap that wasn't the hammer of the Old Man and the Kid, but one that held its own authority. Sophie came out of the kitchen, holding a spatula, her eyes moving to the door then to me, concern clearly ramping up to panic on her face.

I held out a hand, palm facing her, signaling her to stop. I checked Cheryl, who was still sleeping, and got up. Proceeding to the door, I gestured for Sophie to get back into the kitchen, which she did. I gripped

One Sore Rib

the door handle, took a deep breath, trying to clear my head and get my thoughts straight. Then I opened it.

Verdicchio stood outside it, flanked behind by two men that, to his credit, weren't the Old Man and the Kid. Now that we weren't sitting I could tell that Verdicchio was nearly a full head shorter than me. Besides that, though, there was something unsettling about his appearance. In the early morning all three men seemed like they had been up for long hours. Dressed in the casually elegant way only Italians can pull off, their suits had been worn for too long, collars and ties undone, jackets not sitting on their shoulders quite right. A thin film of sweat covered their faces and hair. The man to the right of Verdicchio, a fat white man with a buzz cut and eyes that were too close together, had one of his shoes untied.

But after a pass over all three of them I kept my eyes on the Don. I'd seen men who had been awake past their limits with the kind of insanity that can crawl into the eyes and Verdicchio had it. He hid it well but it was there, in the shiny layer of scum that covered his face, to the breath that smelled like something rotten, to the sunglasses he wore in a dark hall in the early light of morning. I was glad that I had opened the door just enough to stick my head and shoulders out.

His thin frame shook the bedraggled suit from deep within it as he spoke, "Ciao." The friendliness from our first meeting was gone, allowing a sinister dorsal fin to poke itself out of his composure.

"Hiya," keeping it casual myself, trying not to let my eyes go wide with the fear that I felt at taking in all these details. A moment passed in which we both said nothing. I stayed calm and still, waiting. This became increasingly difficult as each passing second of my nothing irritated Verdicchio until he ruffled his suit even more.

"I am here to see Sophie," he said finally, his mouth twisting.

"Right," I said, "of course," sliding back behind the protective cover of the door. "Let me see if she's in" I added stupidly. I kept my eyes on him until I clicked the door shut.

Turning around I could already see Sophie, still standing in the kitchen, spatula in hand, shaking her head with eyes wide and full of panic. Feeling my own fear crowd in on me I thought she might make a break for the window, but I calmed both of us the best I could with a raised hand.

I took a few seconds to think. After those seconds I took a few more to gather some things, quietly rushing around the apartment, feeling Sophie's eyes on me. Arriving back at the door, I composed myself, then opened it.

"Is she here?" Verdicchio asked, the sarcasm in his tone denoting the hope that I wasn't about to tell him another lie.

"Of course," I smiled, trying to sound self-deprecating.

"Good," he smiled more easily at this news. He raised his right hand from his side, pointing straight down with his index finger, "Send her downstairs."

I felt that command stiffen my resolve. "No."

"Excuse me?" His eyes narrowed behind the sunglasses.

"She doesn't want to see you." No eye widening now, no shoulder shrug, just Horatius squaring off on the bridge.

Insulted, Verdicchio drew himself up, head going back, shoulders widening. "Signori, I asked you to protect her. Not to keep her from me."

"She doesn't want to see you." I shook my head,

eyes still on him. "It's early. She's tired," I offered, a small token for his pride.

"This is not what I am paying you for." Real anger now, just below the surface.

"You're right," I said, knowing it would come down to this. I closed the door. Opening it again a moment later Verdiccio radiated confidence, sure that I had capitulated and was about to offer up Sophie. Instead I pushed the envelope out toward him, still filled with most of his Euros.

"Here you go," other hand firmly on the doorknob, ready to snap it shut. "I'll have to get the rest of it back to you later."

I actually surprised the old son of a bitch. I'd be lying if I said I didn't take some pleasure in that. I watched it pull him between anger and the desire not to lose his cool. Even in his haggard state, his dignity and pride won out.

He reached out, crumpling the front of the envelope, turning it back towards me. "No, you keep it my friend." Letting go of it, he stepped back. "I will return some time at a more proper hour."

I nodded, trying to appear confused and conciliatory at the same time. "Sure thing."

I waited until Verdicchio and his two disappeared below the horizon of the stairs before I closed the door. Inside, I took a deep breath leaning back against the door and set the envelope on the pedestal next to it, along with the KA-BAR. After I could tear my eyes away from the ceiling, I saw Sophie, still at the kitchen door, staring at me expectantly. I nodded, "They're gone."

Her panic, which she had been holding in place the entire time, broke into a wave of gratitude which carried her across the room and into my chest with a hug. I held her there, her babbling more than enough thanks. She finally spun herself out and let go of me, giving me a kiss on the cheek, and bounced back into the kitchen to finish cooking breakfast. I sighed, trying not to let the void the adrenaline was leaving behind get filled with worry and fear about the future.

I realized I couldn't succeed, so I grabbed the KA-BAR and found my whetstone. When Cheryl woke up, I was sitting on the couch at her feet, sharpening the knife.

"What's wrong?" she asked.

"Nothing," I replied, not taking my eyes off the blade.

Chapter 16

"You're a horrible liar," Cheryl said to me later. Her voice was thick with fatigue and her eyes had trouble focusing, but she could see right through me.

"Only to you," I smiled, kneading the foot that I had placed on my lap as we sat on the couch. In exchange for muting the television (even now some over-exuberant young woman bounced around a smiling old man playing to the audience, I'd buy that for a dollar) I had agreed to give her a foot massage. I would have done it just to see her enjoy a physical sensation, but getting rid of the babbling box for a while was icing on the cake. Sophie was somewhere else, probably reading in her bedroom or using the bath, but for some reason I imagined her sunbathing on the roof. Given the rain pattering against the windows that was unlikely, but the image stuck anyway.

"Or when you tell a lie with a knife in your hand. What happened earlier?" Cheryl craned her neck in an attempt to indicate the door, but didn't get very far. But it told me that she had been awake enough to hear some of what happened.

"Verdicchio dropped by." I tried to make it sound casual.

"Oh? For a cup of sugar?" Another lie spotted, shot down. Dragging me into a conversation I didn't want to have, it made me smile anyway. I pushed a retaliatory thumb a little too hard into the arch of her foot, eliciting an 'Ow' and a weak kick back.

"No," I said, the smile fading, "he wanted to see Sophie."

Cheryl's blurry eyes locked onto me, concern

showing through the fog of pain and painkillers. "What did he want with her?"

"He didn't say. But he didn't want to come in – he wanted me to send her downstairs." I chose not to look at Cheryl as I said this, paying attention to her foot. If I could help it I didn't want her to see the worry in my own eyes. Another pointless exercise. She had already caught it or we wouldn't be having the conversation.

"For sex?" Direct and without tact.

"Probably." That bothered me enough, but wouldn't have been out of the bounds of normalcy. And it probably wouldn't have been enough for me to endanger Cheryl as we tried to find some peace in that tiny lagoon at the end of our lives.

Cheryl gripped one of my fingers between her big and second toes, pulling my eyes back to hers, her expression clearer now, more concerned. "What is it?"

"What?" I shrugged, feeling insecurity boil up, worried that Cheryl could see that my protectiveness of Sophie had gone beyond chivalry, if it had ever been that. "I can't get bent out of shape because he wants me to be a pimp?" I felt the same urge to run that had almost overcome me when Sophie had shown up on the roof in her nightgown.

"Of course you can," another pull on my finger, this time with affection. "But there's more to it than that."

I kept kneading her feet, slowing as I thought. I eventually came to a stop completely, leaning back into the couch and staring out the window, thinking about a place that was filled with sun and blasted heat and dust instead of clouds and rain. Cheryl only watched me, waiting for me to form my answer.

"I've seen men stay awake for days," I finally started. "Boys too," I offered as an afterthought.

Cheryl used her shoulder blades to walk back on the couch, trying to pull herself upright. I asked her, "You remember Brian?"

"Sure. He was at our wedding."

"In high school sometimes me and him would get ahold of some speed or meth and we'd stay awake for days. Days," I emphasized the last word trying to remember something that felt like it happened a very long time ago. "Then in the Corps there were times we'd have to stay awake for what felt like weeks." I gave Cheryl a level gaze to make the distinction between high school hijinks and serious business. "No one does that on their own, but no one ever used anything stupid," meaning illegal, "but we'd chew tobacco by the handful, drink energy drinks by the gallon. Some guys would even eat instant coffee grounds right out of the packets."

I could tell by the quizzical expression on Cheryl's face that I was losing her. "The point is, I've seen men stay awake for days. Verdicchio looked a lot like that when he came up here."

More confusion from Cheryl. "I don't think..."

I patted her leg, a signal to let me continue. She did. "Some guys do it because they have to, some because they need to. Some guys do it because they think it's fun."

I paused, then continued, "But almost all of them, at some point, if they do it long enough, get mean. And when they get mean, they like to hurt things. The worst of them like to hurt people."

"Like Sophie," Cheryl said, drawing her own conclusion.

"Like Sophie," I repeated in confirmation. "She probably got into bed with him because he was nice at first." The unintentional pun got me another kick. "He can be a real charmer," I offered in consolation from my own experience. "But I suspect after awhile he got mean and just kept getting meaner and now she's hiding with us."

Cheryl lifted her gaze up the stairs and I stared at her, both of us more worried than ever. It never occurred to Cheryl that I might be concerned about her. That just showed the cancer couldn't rob Cheryl of what made her beautiful, not capable of taking it all even now. So I sincerely doubted Verdicchio could. At least not without resorting to that final step that would rob Cheryl of everything and I doubted Verdicchio was stupid enough to do that. He didn't strike me as the type to enjoy Pyrrhic victories.

Coming back to me Cheryl asked, "So what now?"

I had been thinking about that since Verdicchio left, but took another moment to consider the options. "He'll either come and try to take her or ask for something else. If he asks for something else and I can, I'll need to give it to him. That might ease the hurt in his pride. But God knows what he'd asked for."

"Could he really ask for that much?"

"I don't know," honesty caused me to shrug my shoulders. "I'm not sure what he's capable of. Either I've got him wrong or he exercised a monstrous amount of restraint this morning. I mean, most guys would probably have started frothing at the mouth if I pulled on them what I did with Verdicchio."

"Does she have a passport? We could use his money to put her on a plane and send her somewhere new."

I thought about that, enjoying the humor in it. But truthfully I said, "I didn't see one when I was moving her stuff. If she does have one I don't know how far she'd get. She only speaks Italian, she wouldn't have any prospects wherever we sent her, and Verdicchio is the type of guy that could figure out where she'd gone." I thought about Verdicchio's mentioning of Castardi and shuddered a little internally.

"So we wait," Cheryl said in a small voice.

"Yeah."

Cheryl reached out for my hand and I took hers, entwining her fingers with my own. She gave me a squeeze so I felt her bones and in the same quiet voice she said, "We can't keep her safe here forever."

"Yeah." I squeezed her hand back. I reached for the remote with the other hand to turn up the volume on the television.

Chapter 17

Little by little Sophie eventually took over the responsibility of feeding Cheryl along with preparing meals for herself and me. It was a welcome change, Sophie being better in the kitchen than Cheryl and I ever were, even if you combined our culinary skills. It didn't matter to Cheryl though, who hardly ever used her food to do more than choke down pain pills and so grew more skeletal by the day. Sophie didn't take Cheryl's lack of enthusiasm for her food personally, but she did spend a lot of time hovering in the kitchen door watching Cheryl to see if she'd eat.

Rather than the pat exercise it had become for me, whipping up the slurry was an endless experiment in Sophie's hands. The grocery list that she sent me out with was always changing, a never ceasing combination of fruits, yogurts, and nuts. Given my Italian hadn't improved any more than Sophie's English (our intermittent lessons hadn't gotten far) it made each shopping trip into a minor adventure that offered me a welcome distraction.

It also provided me with more opportunities to speak with the smiling old orange merchant with the permanent shades. I asked him for assistance when I came across something on the list that I didn't recognize. The market was filled with produce, big and small, much of which I didn't know the English names for, so this was a pretty regular occurrence. Regular enough that I learned his name was Alonzo and that he wasn't Italian, but originally from Seville. He had come to Italy for a woman a long time ago and I suppose we had that in common.

I was leaning in close enough to smell the

cigarettes and wine on his breath, showing him another mystery fruit on the list, when I felt him go cold. I lifted my eyes from the list to his face and even with his sunglasses on I could see him giving the stink-eye to someone behind me. I peered over my shoulder, but didn't see anything. Looking down, I saw Dennis.

"G'day, mate." Dennis did not, in fact, appear to be having a good day. He was even more scruffy and rough than usual, almost as if he'd been sleeping outside for a few nights, the blue jeans and oilskin coat he wore rumpled and dirty. He didn't smile and whatever glimmer of merriment had been in his eyes was now flinty. People walking through the market gave him a wide berth, floating around him on unseen eddies.

Turning back to Alonzo I asked, "How's it?"

"Oh," Dennis started to say something then gave a small shrug, one I could feel more than see. "You know."

"I suppose I do." I counted out a few coins, grabbed my bag and faced him. "What can I do for you?"

"I thought you might want to come down to the Mondiale for a drink." I hadn't had a drink since Verdicchio's last visit and I felt a twinge of shame as the back of my brain jumped at the idea.

Instead I just pushed it down and said, "I don't think that's a good idea."

Dennis took his left hand out of his pocket to scratch his nose like this might get rid of the disappointment there. Finished, he said, "I got something for you." He didn't make it sound like something I wanted.

With Dennis standing in the market, hands pushed into the great bulk of his coat, I realized why the Venetians, usually eager to bump and jostle, were stepping around Dennis. There was something of the inevitable about Dennis, as if he possessed his own gravity, and they moved around me and him trying not to get pulled into it.

"Yeah, OK," I said, yielding, "let me drop this stuff off at the apartment and I'll meet you there."

"Probably better to come now before I have to open the doors," he replied casually. "More privacy that way."

"Sure," I said despite the jolt of apprehension that went through me. I started toward the Rialto Bridge, but then turned to a water taxi ("Traghetto," I heard Sophie say) that was docked next to the market and quickly filling up with people wanting to make their way across the canal. I had only ridden on one of the tiny, narrow boats before. Filled with a crowd, particularly when going across the busy traffic of the Grand Canal, they could toss and pitch ominously, threatening to spill all of their passengers into the water. Cheryl hadn't cared for it so we hadn't ridden in one since our arrival, but I was curious to see what Dennis' reaction would be. He jumped into the boat behind me without hesitation.

No matter where you were in Venice you were never far from the water and that was never more true than in a traghetto. The hull of the boat rose only a few inches out of the canal, providing very little protection against the water splashing from the wakes of larger boats. It swayed with the weight of the people in it as well, but the expert hand of the ferryman got us across without any more trouble than wet feet.

Not surprised, but disappointed, I watched Dennis all the way across. Neither the rocking of the boat nor the threat of the cold water caused him any

One Sore Rib

ill affects. We hopped out near the turgid wooden docks of Fondamenta Vin Castello and pushed our way into the thickening morning crowds. We made our way through the narrow network of cobbled streets to the Mondiale.

Almost everything in Venice opened early enough to take advantage of the daytripper economy. Long before the tourists rolled off the first cruise ship of the day nearly everything was open and ready for business, even ancient saloons serving up crepes and waffles to hungry tourists. As we passed by the bright white plastic of a cell phone store filled with the tall colorful advertisements of beautiful people smiling into their new phones, I thought about using some of Verdicchio's cash to buy a burner. But then I thought of the byzantine combinations that formed Italian phone numbers, shook my head and kept walking.

The brown-orange wooden door of the Mondiale stood embedded in the gray stone of the corner the bar inhabited, but unlike everything else around, it was dark through its window. Taking out a jailer's worth of keys Dennis shuffled through them with a professional grace, found the correct one, and opened the door. We stepped into the Mondiale, me having to duck through the entrance.

Inside my eyes began to adjust to the dim light filtering through the windows. The Mondiale didn't feel alive this early – all the action was outside, walking by. In here the dim and quiet made it feel like the room was more museum than bar. The dark wood absorbed what little light there was and the brass fixtures were lackluster, struggling to throw off reflections.

I walked down the length of the bar and stopped at my usual seat, without actually sitting. Dennis swung around to the end and behind the bar to assume his customary position. He reached into the cooler, ice gnashing together as he asked, "Beer?"

"Sure." No hesitation there. I told myself I didn't want to seem ungrateful.

Dennis took out an Urquell and set it on the bar. With it he said, "Verdicchio wants you to do something for him."

I picked up the green bottle and drank from it, pursing my lips as I swallowed. I didn't bother trying to fake surprise. "What's that?"

"He wants you to go over to Marghera and take care of something." I could see that whatever happiness Dennis got from tending bar was gone. His speech was clipped and without tone, his frame didn't move with the same animation that he had when serving patrons or watching soccer. I crushed a small piece of me that started to feel sorry for him.

"Marghera's on the other side of the lagoon?"

"On the mainland, yeah."

"Can't do it," I set down the beer, not wanting to appear too eager. "You know my situation."

Dennis went about doing his prep work, avoiding eye contact. "It's 10 minutes by train, an evening's work. You'll be back before you know it." He stopped then and looked at me like a storyteller getting to the interesting bit, "And it pays."

I raised my eyebrows at that, reached out and took the bottle in hand, running my thumb across the neck label, contemplating it. Or at least trying to create the impression that I was contemplating it, pretending I had a choice. "What's he want done?"

Dennis reached behind the bar like I'd seen him do a dozen times to grab a fresh glass or a lime. This time though he came up with a black pistol. He laid it flat so the grip was facing me and the barrel was pointed to the door. The oversized trigger guard and insignia told me it was an M9, like an old familiar friend you recognize from across the room.

I didn't touch it. "Beretta. That's appropriate."

Dennis shrugged. "Italians know their way around a weapon."

"What's it for?"

Dennis enshrined the pistol by placing his hands palm down on either side of it. "There's a stickybeak across the pond, needs discouraging."

I picked up the gun, felt the weight of it. "It's not loaded."

"You won't need it to be."

I was relieved by that, although I still would have preferred to have ammunition if I was going to take the risk of carrying the pistol. But I just said, "OK."

"Beauty."

Chapter 18

Standing on the cobblestones of Cannaregio I stared out over the weathered, black gondolas, across the lagoon, all the way to Marghera. At this distance the neighboring municipality might as well have been an entirely different world, something out of a disparate time.

The Marghera horizon was dominated by the long necks of cranes, the hulls of industrial ships, and the stacks of refineries. It gave the impression of it being something unhealthy and swollen, bristling with spines, leaking solvents and fuels into the calm waters it shared with *La Serenissima*. I knew that was unfair though. A place as stubbornly unchanging as the island of Venice couldn't survive without a place like Marghera, a place for the hard work and dirty laundry, a place with an eye towards the future. Or at least the present.

I walked south on Calle Carmelitani till I passed the Church of the Scalzi and came to the train station. The two couldn't have been a better contrast. The church was ornate in its decoration, its white marble surface covered with sculptures and statues, all of it incredibly well preserved. The train station was white and old as well, and clean with no litter around, but the white was tinged with brown dirt like a smoker's teeth. Not old like the church, but disused. It felt like something thrown up by people who had never really wanted it and now it stuck into the island of Venice like a mechanical hand.

I bought a ticket to Marghera on the 7:10 train out of a boxy machine. Its grainy screen would have fit right in at one of the arcades that hadn't existed since

One Sore Rib

I was in middle school. Now they only lived in tourist towns like Manitou Springs. I paused at that, thinking of a trip Cheryl and I had taken to Pike's Peak a long time ago. I remembered her smiling as we walked through the maze of man-high machines, stacked side by side like some sort of museum to my youth. I almost threw the ticket away then, but thought of Sophie when I had left. She had been curled up next to Cheryl on our bed like an exhausted child or lover. She looked like she felt safe.

I put the ticket in my pocket and walked to the regional train that was headed for Porto Marghera. Lined up next to the sleek bullet trains, the commuter one was a brick, a double-decker with a blunt nose and alternating blue and white stripes. I'm sure I stood out as an American, but the banality of the train made me feel anonymous. I climbed aboard to Marghera with my hood pulled low, trying to obscure my face as best I could.

It almost wasn't necessary. The train was nearly empty. There were three other men on the car I sidled into, one in an orange construction safety vest, another in a soccer club hoodie, and one in a gray, expensively cut suit, each of them tired and ready to be somewhere else. I sat down on a hard plastic chair, stared out the window and fit right in.

A speaker squawked something so garbled that I doubt I could have understood even if I spoke Italian. With a perceptible lurch the train started to move forward, pulling out on the gray fingers of the rail station and towards the lagoon. The inside lights of the train and the headlights of the cars running parallel on the Ponte della Libertà made everything else outside into a dark unknown. I wished for a moment that I had left earlier during the day so I could see the water. As it was, the window only reflected my own face and the dull yellow interior of the car, leaving me alone with my doubts.

While I had told Cheryl that this job was penance for denying access to Sophie, I figured it was more likely a convenient way for Verdicchio to kill two birds with one stone. I'd go to Marghera, pull off this job, take care of his problem person, then get picked up somewhere with the gun and spend some time in an Italian jail. Maybe gum up the judicial works waiting for extradition. Too much time for the women to be on their own, plenty of time for Verdicchio to stroll in with his grandfatherly ways and offer support that couldn't be refused. Sophie would be taken someplace with whispered promises that Cheryl would be cared for, when she'd probably be dumped in the nearest lagoon. I figured if I pulled off the job and didn't get caught then Verdicchio wouldn't be able to complain and I'd have bought me and the women a little more time. And the way things were progressing, a little more time was all we needed.

The train broke from the ocean to the land with a minute change in the cabin pressure that felt like being in a fast car as it comes out of a tunnel. The silhouetted landscape out the window didn't change much, still dark despite sprouting more lights from its oblong and rectangular shapes.

The loudspeaker squawked again and the train began to slow. I felt myself panic slightly as all three of the other travelers made preparations to leave, picking up briefcase shaking awake, pulling hood back up. Wondering if I missed something, feeling the pull of the others, I checked my ticket as if it would hold some magic answer. But it didn't and I held my place as the rest shuffled off. I was rewarded for my patience a few minutes later, the speaker crackling out more nonsense, but some of which I caught as "Porto

One Sore Rib

Marghera."

The train stop for Marghera didn't look like it belonged in Italy. Or anywhere in the First World. I stepped out onto an island under a cement canopy that was held up by square pillars, lit by a single incandescent light and the glow of a monitor displaying train times. I should have paid more attention to that, but that was then.

Across two sets of tracks sat an ugly, slanted building that was the same dead concrete color as the pillars. Its windows were dark and the doors shuttered, making it look like an East German bunker. On its tallest side, facing the island I was on, hung a blue sign covered in graffiti, announcing that I had indeed arrived at Porto Marghera. I crossed over the tracks to make sure the place was empty, but the only sound were the fans spinning on some dilapidated cooling units. I did find a map, though, hung in a protective metal and plastic case. Through the scratches and gouges on the plastic's surface I was able to determine my location and verify my route. I glanced around, tried to feel lucky about how empty this place was, and then set off north, taking a bridge over the tracks and nearby road.

Out past the train station I was surprised how quickly the landscape broke into green. Behind the industry that separated Venice from the residents of Marghera were well-tended lawns and rows of small, neat houses. Most of them were uniform in size with white walls and terracotta roofs. As I walked through the neighborhood I felt panic try to put its tentacles around me. The similarities of the houses, unmarred by the decay of Venice or the disfigurements of the train station, made navigating to my destination that much more difficult. I had considered coming out during the day to walk the path I had charted in an internet cafe the day before. I had rejected this idea, though, unwilling to leave Cheryl and Sophie for a moment longer than necessary, and not willing to double the exposure of someone seeing me and being able to identify me later.

I regretted that now, fumbling around in the dark like some pedophile in a nice neighborhood. I found myself walking briskly from streetlamp to streetlamp hoping no one in those houses would look out and see this stranger in their midst.

I began to wonder if I had been given the wrong address and a dozen other questions came up with it, the ropes of panic continuing to squeeze my brain. Then I saw it – a late model Fiat parked out on the street in front of one of the homes. I checked the house to confirm the address was correct. It was.

The windows of the house were lit with the same orange glow that most of the homes in the neighborhood were, but more noise issued forth. A party or family dinner, maybe. There was only one car outside though, which allowed me to put aside concerns about other guests. I scanned the street. Certain as I could be that it was empty, I walked over to the car.

I took the key that Dennis had given me out of my pocket and breathed a sigh of relief when it fit into the Fiat's lock. I popped open one of the car's two doors as quietly as I could and slid into the back.

Whoever had come up with the original plan of ambush by rear seat must have conceived it back in the '50s when seats in cars were like couches laid out in bathtubs. The Fiat was a much tighter squeeze, having to crunch my body just to fit into it. Hiding, even in the dark, parked as it was away from any streetlamps, was going to be impossible. If the car's owner should glance into the backseat while getting into the car I imagined it would be hard to miss me. I wriggled and writhed, my anxiousness growing by each minute that I spent trying to cram my knees or my shoulders behind the horizon of the car's front seats. Feeling like a giant trying to fit into a clown car it occurred to me that Dennis must have thought of this plan with his own small frame in mind. It wasn't going to work for me.

Popping my head up like some kind of trapped meerkat, I looked around to make sure that no one had appeared on the street. Once I had confirmed there wasn't, I unstuffed myself from between the seats, leaned the seat forward and wriggled out of the car. Surveying the street again and finding it still vacant, I quickly put the seat back and tried to rearrange the car's interior to how I had found it.

Out of the car, I located a dark spot next to some trash bins from which I could observe the Fiat and close the distance to the driver's side in some quick steps. There, I wiped the perspiration out of my eyes and realized the ordeal of the tiny car and the threat of getting caught had caused my entire body to become covered in sweat. I laughed, knowing I had sweated less with much more on the line, but then checked that – if I screwed up here then Cheryl and Sophie would be on their own. That was a lot more important than catching a bullet in the brain in some desert no one cared about.

I was playing that through my head, cursing myself for not having a better plan other than reacting to Verdicchio's. Then I saw the man I was waiting for step out of the house I was watching. The red front door opened and he appeared, an elderly couple in tow. He was tall and slight, with the same wavy dark hair from the photograph Dennis had shown me. He wore a loose cut white button-down shirt and, what

I'm sure, were an expensive pair of trousers and shoes.

The way he and the elderly couple entangled and disentangled from each other in a series of good-bye kisses and hugs made it clear that they were his parents. Like I imagined many parents who don't see their children often enough, they stood by the front door waving at him as he crossed their small lawn to his car. I breathed a sigh of relief and thanked whatever god was listening when they went back inside.

He was fumbling with his keys, most likely about to engage in Italy's national sport of drunk driving. Distracted as he was, I walked up behind him. Grabbing him by the back of his collar I straight-armed his chest and head into the side of the car, his body landing with a heavy thud and a hollow echo. He began to protest, so I did it again. Keeping him pinned there, feeling angry heat start to come off him, I showed him the gun. He stopped struggling.

"Get in the car." I was lucky in that he understood English. His anger transformed into fear, he fumbled with his keys for a completely different reason. He managed to open the door. We began an awkward waltz of me trying to maneuver us into the car while keeping him in front of me, trying to minimize how much he saw of my face. Once he had the door open I pulled him around to face away from the car as I popped the backseat forward and crouched backwards into the rear. I dragged him with me as I went, pulling him into the front seat after using my pistol hand to click the seat back into position. I'm sure in a different time and place it probably would have been hilarious.

I ordered him to close the door and he did. He started to speak again so I cracked him on the back of the skull with the butt of the pistol and said, "Drive." He was shaking so bad that he dropped his keys onto the floor mat while trying to put them into the ignition. I let him go so he could bend down to search for them. I spent those nervous moments watching the front door of his parents' house hoping that they didn't come out to see what was wrong.

Eventually Shaky got the car started and we began to move. I kept the directions simple with lefts and rights, steering us south out of the neighborhood through the industrial zone to a piece of the lagoon that was isolated, Dennis had assured me, due to its use for toxic runoff. It seemed to take longer than I expected, though, which got me thinking about catching the train back. By the time I told Shaky to stop the car I felt as nervous as he looked.

The gun had never been far from his head during the trip but now I put it up to his temple, squeezing the muzzle against him so there could be no doubt as to what it was. I ordered him to throw the keys and his phone out the window. They disappeared somewhere into the lagoon with a wet plop.

I pulled back the hammer on the pistol. When he started to pray I pulled the trigger.

The click of the hammer was enough to cause him to jump. Realizing he wasn't dead he began to hyperventilate and tremble violently, his head bowing to the driver's wheel. I reached over the chair to grip him by his neck again, pulling him to sit up straight. "Mind your own business." I was so close as I delivered the message I could smell his aftershave, sweat, and fear. I slammed him into the steering wheel, then pinned him there by flipping the seat up.

Getting out of the car I could see the area was dimly lit by the light from a distant refinery, high and bright like a magnesium flare. I took a moment to orient myself. Then I threw the pistol into the lagoon and ran off into the night.

Chapter 19

It began to rain on my way back to the train station. Even though each minute I had spent in the car seemed to be translating into hours on foot, I didn't want to run. It might draw attention to me and whatever else Shaky already knew, he knew I was an American and that was already too much. If a crazy loner got stopped out in the middle of nowhere it wouldn't take much to connect the dots. So I kept moving and got off the road if any traffic came along.

When I saw the arch of the overpass near the station, though, my restraint crumbled away and I broke into a jog. I came to a panting stop at the Port Marghera bunker, checking around to see if I could find a schedule. I found it on the monitor hanging under the canopy and instantly became glad that I hadn't attracted any attention on the way back. The reflection on the screen showed a man slick with rain and fear, unshaven and exhausted. I looked like one of those crazed 'Nam vets out of the movies I watched as a kid.

I pushed past that to view the mostly blank screen. The few lines of green text showed that the last train had left at midnight. Checking my watch I cursed to see that I had only missed it by a few minutes. The next one wouldn't be till morning.

That didn't change the situation though, so I started evaluating my options. I thought about trying to find a taxi but, if somehow I could at this time of night, a lone American catching a ride back to the island would surely stick in the memory of the driver. But then I remembered the crowds of people huddling onto waterbuses ("Vaporetto," I heard Sophie say) and wondered if those were still running. It was unlikely given how dead Venice was in the late hours, but it was better than doing nothing. I started hiking south towards the shoreline.

If the car had converted hours into minutes, the train had made them into seconds. It didn't take long before walking to the shore became an interminable slog, made worse by the lack of recognizable landmarks to mark progress. In the darker spots I checked the stars to make sure I was still headed in the right direction. The rest of the time I tried not to think.

The sun started to come up and the rain had mostly stopped by the time I was close to the shore. Scanning the horizon for some sign of the ocean meant I wasn't paying enough attention to my footing. I slipped and dropped into a small canal. Like many of the earthen canals near the shore, this one was formed by two sloping berms with water flowing between them. I stumbled down like a man missing a stair. My knee buckled and I barely caught myself with the other foot, landing me in a genuflect position hip deep in water. I let out a string of curses that only continued as I slipped trying to right myself, sinking me back in. From my position in soggy bottom I glanced up and down the canal. I didn't see a bridge or any other means of crossing it. Already soaked, I decided to trudged across, swearing all the while.

Pulling myself up the face of the opposite berm, my cursing dwindled off as I tried to shake the briny water from my clothes. In front of me, a small wooden dock stretched out into the lagoon. On it stood a black-capped man, winding up one of the tethering lines from a blue-hulled boat, looking at me with what appeared to be a mix of amusement and worry. I must have been quite a sight.

He called to me in Italian leaving no doubt that I had been spotted. I walked down the exterior of the canal, paying attention to my feet this time. I gave the man an awkward smile and wave, preparing to walk away, hoping he'd forget about me later. Instead he dropped the line and crossed the dock speaking to me in what were obvious overtures of concern. As he got closer I could see he was elderly, not like Old Man old, but actually advanced in years, with tan working coveralls over thermals to go with his black cap. He smiled as he got closer, revealing gaps in his teeth, scratching at the gray hair between his ear and cap.

I just tried to blink the fatigue out of my eyes and mumbled excuses in English. I ended with, "I'm just trying to get back to the island," gesturing towards Venice, which I gratefully noted I could at least now see. His smile widened at that as he clapped a hand on my shoulder with impressive force, gesturing happily towards his boat. I blinked again for completely different reasons and raised my hands, trying to make a flattered refusal to a deeply generous offer. He just smiled more, squeezed my shoulder, and guided me towards the boat. With him leading I walked across the dock in a bit of a daze until he brought me to the bow where he gestured for me to get in. I boarded as he gave me encouraging words, clearly gratified I could get into the boat without falling into the water.

While he brought in the last tethering line from its cleat I sat in the bow and stared down the boat's centerline at its contents – a round cage, lots of rope, netting, a few poles with hooks on the ends. He walked behind the tiny cabin at the rear, every inch the fisherman he clearly was. I felt strangely comforted by this. With an old familiarity he put the boat out into the lagoon. I slumped behind the gunwale and felt the gentle rocking of the water.

One Sore Rib

While I fought against the heaviness of my eyelids I could see him smiling at me from the cabin, probably thinking that I was just another young man who had gotten drunk and in trouble on the mainland. I didn't have any problem imagining him doing something like that in his own youth.

The clunk of the boat against something woke me. Arching my back against the interior of the bow, I peaked over the gunwale to see the fisherman had docked us at a stone pier. Raising my eyes from the perfect, flat geometry of the pier I saw another one of the impressive churches of Venice, a white-domed cathedral with a rising brown stone tower. Attached to the church was a stone wall the same color as the tower, stretching out along the pier. All of it bobbed up and down with the gentle rocking of the boat.

Seeing no one around, I picked myself up and prepared to jump out of the boat with a quick thank you and good-bye to the fisherman. But I couldn't bring myself to do it. Instead I grabbed a tethering line and hopped onto the pier, securing the bow while he did the same at the stern. Before I could think of a way to thank him, I glanced out across the water.

Both impossibly far away and just out of reach the island of Venice rose out of the lagoon in the distance. From here, for the first time, I realized Venice wasn't as gray as I had thought, trapped inside it. Many of the buildings were painted bright, irregular colors making it stand out against the sky and water that blended together behind it. If I hadn't dozed off on the way back it would have been impossible to miss.

I quickly finished tying up the boat and hustled over to the fisherman who was shortening his rope. He must have seen the horror on my face as I came over because he was already holding up his hands, rope still between them, palms towards me, making slow-down motions. I started talking anyway, gesturing towards the island, but he just kept pushing his palms to the ground and pulling them up again, repeating this, giving me a few seconds to bluster myself out.

When I had he shrugged in an apologetic way and gestured toward an arched opening in the stone wall indicating he had some business beyond. With a tap on his wristwatch he added it wouldn't take long. He spouted a string of Italian that would have mollified a less desperate man while backing across the pier and through the arch, shrugging and gesturing the entire way towards whatever destination he had beyond.

I followed him with widening eyes until he passed through the arch, some part of me still not believing he was leaving me here, desperate to get back to Cheryl. Another part of me was incredulous that I was giving him grief after showing me such extraordinary kindness. I swung back to the gray lagoon and the colorful Venice shoreline and tried to think of what to do.

My eye prowled up the length of the fishing boat as I thought about stealing it. I shook that off along with the shame the idea brought on. I went back to the lagoon, watching the early morning traffic stitch its way back and forth in front of the city, each boat leaving a white trail in its wake. I waited for awhile hoping that a water taxi would land on the pier so I could hop a ride back to Venice. After a few minutes, though, I lost what little patience I had left and followed the fisherman through the arch.

The short tunnel led out into the church's courtyard, a square open area that's stone floor was a brilliant white, contrasting to the dark, mottled yellows and reds of its walls. The moment I stepped in I felt more out of place than I had in any other time while in Italy. Trying my best to be quiet, I still felt clumsy and loud in the ethereal silence of the courtyard. There were no crowds here either, just a group of men near the church, each dressed in white shirts and black pants, standing around a long, black shape that stood at table height. They took the cigarettes out of their mouths long enough to give me unwelcoming stares, sizing me up for no apparent reason. Staring back I realized the oblong shape they surrounded was a coffin. Mortified at the idea that I might be interrupting a funeral I left quickly through one of the many other arches that punctuated the courtyard's walls.

The gate I took let out into another open courtyard, a stone half-circle surrounded by pillars of the same white stone. The arches between the columns were large enough to see that there was green grass and more white stone just beyond. This appeared to be the most Roman structure I had seen anywhere around Venice, with no flourishes or decorations or exaltations to God or church, just a practical construction leading from one part of the island to the next. It felt incongruous to the rest of the Republic and disorienting. Standing in place I spun, following the perimeter of the half-circle, trying to figure out which stone arch the old fisherman had gone. With no real clue I picked randomly and went.

Coming out the other side, for a moment I thought I had been transported to Arlington. Stretching out in front of me to the horizon, with white markers in uniform green spaces, were burial plots. The silence of the church courtyard solidified here, trapping time like a fly in amber. I swept my eyes across the landscape, realizing that this was the rest of the island, a place dedicated to the dead, a floating mausoleum, a cemetery ship.

Unsure of what to do or where to go I picked one of the many rows that radiated out from the courtyard and started down it. Walking among the graves I realized that they weren't as uniform as I had thought. While most were the same pure shade of white as the courtyard I had just come from, their geometry was different, some straight and simple and plain, others ornate like small churches or temples. Small offerings had also been laid at many, flowers or red ribbons placed in small bronze cups flanking each marker.

I wandered through the grid that the tombstones made, sticking to the stone path, respect and superstition keeping me off the grass. Spotting the fisherman I stopped a few dozen meters away as he was gathered at a marker with others. The rest of them, a man, woman, and two small children, were dressed in black, fine in their Sunday best. All of them had their heads bowed, hands clasped before them praying at the tombstone. I kept my distance to let them finish paying their respects. Eventually, they made the sign of the cross in unison, the two small children fumbling through the ritual. That tugged at me, the sensation only growing as the old fisherman was embraced by each of his family in turn.

Restrained from running by forces I didn't understand, I retreated from the scene at a fast clip. Unable to resist the urge to peek back over my shoulder though, I saw the old fisherman continue to hug what could only be his children and grandchildren. A voice in my head hounded me away with the cruel words, "You'll never have that."

Nestled in the ship's bow I had managed to regain most of my composure by the time the fisherman had returned. He smiled warmly, rejuvenated with a spring in his step, and waved at seeing me still there. I smiled and hoped he didn't notice any difference in my state. He didn't and we put out into the lagoon.

Chapter 20

Traversing the lagoon from the northern small island to Venice meant cutting across the growing early morning boat traffic. It all headed east or west while we went south, which made for a bumpy ride. I've never prone to seasickness but I still had some trouble keeping my teeth in my head until we hit the island's "no wake" zone: An imaginary boundary around it where boats were meant to slow their speeds as not to give off the large waves that were at least partially responsible for Venice's erosion. Like most laws, though, the locals either ignored it outright or skirted it, but the decrease in speed of outsiders made the remainder of the trip a bit smoother.

The fisherman eventually put us into a large marina that looked as if it might have functioned as some kind of defense network in earlier times. The outer portion of it was a seawall with a tower at the corner, making it impossible for him to just drop me off at the bank. He took me into the interior with the same smile he had been wearing since we left the other isle. The inside of the marina only reinforced the impression of it being some left over fortification, as old and maze-like as the rest of Venice. The modern and well-maintained sail and powerboats in the marina were the only thing that kept it from looking like something out of the Renaissance.

The fisherman pulled his boat up to the rickety and worn gray boards of the dock and I stepped off without him needing to stop and tether the boat. Behind the glass window of his small cabin he waved with one hand as he spun the wheel with the other, reversing the boat and disappearing back into the lagoon.

It felt like Venice would sink into the ocean before I finished walking the perimeter of the marina to the exit. I found myself resisting the urge to break into a run. I knew I was on the northern part of the island and that the apartment was near the southern but I didn't know any more than that. Once out of the marina all I could do was find a canal street heading south and follow it.

Like all things in Venice, following the path into the island eventually led to the Grand Canal, now seemingly wider than it had been before. I fidgeted along it for awhile, moving west to follow the canal's elliptical, trying to find a bridge across it. Then, when I could, I headed south to try and go around it. This serpentine route started to feel like the worst of both decisions, taking more time than either following the canal or trying to head directly south. I opted for a third choice, finding a vaporetto station.

The stations for waterbuses in Venice were strange affairs, flimsy things that bobbed in the wake of the Grand Canal, giving the impression they might sink at any moment. Made of skeletal steel and boxed in transparent glass with strange carpet that covered much of the floor, their ticket machines resembled old ATMs. All of this gave each station an amusement park feel, so much so I half-expected a fake shark to pop up out of the water as I ran up the ramp.

If I was reading the schedule right, the vaporetto boarding at this station was headed to the stop near Saint Mark's, near the apartment. I quickly bought a ticket and shot past an attendant holding a rope barrier along the entrance of the boat.

Vaporettos have a lot in common with their land-based cousins, being slow and large, designed to hold as many people as possible. I made my way to the bow, agonizing over the S-shaped progress it made through the island bouncing as it did from one side of the canal to the other, stopping at the stations on either side. The vaporetto finally came to St. Mark's and I nearly hopped off the bow.

Running in Venice is generally frowned upon – it attracts attention at the very least. Normally there are too many people in too small a space for such athletics. There's something about the Italian cool it upsets and, if you're running, you can feel the eyes of *La Serenissima* upon you, following with disapproval. I ran anyway, through the crowds on narrow walkways by canals, dodging past people in the square, past the 'I Love Tourism' office. I got to our door in such a hurry that for a second I was sure I had lost my keys somewhere on the journey. But I hadn't needed to worry about that. The door was open.

The entrance from the alley hadn't quite locked, not pulled securely shut by the last person to use it. As I pushed through the door and ran up the stairs to apartment #5 some part of my brain tried to futilely tell me that the invisible woman in apartment #1 had just forgot to close it behind her. It was heavy and she was old and hadn't bothered.

All of that evaporated the moment I hit the top of the stairs and saw the wreckage of the door there. I stood, unable to comprehend the scene of the heavy door splintered off its hinges. I stared at it dumbly and said, "The son of a bitch brought a battering ram." Then I ran inside.

Nothing on the couch, so up the stairs I flew with the jangling of the wires, ducking my head at the top, through the bedroom door, sliding to the side of the bed on my knees when I saw Cheryl there. She was laid out, legs and arms straight, head toward the ceiling. She or Sophie had wrapped a bandana around her head to keep it warm in the night. I grabbed her hand and kissed it then kissed her face. Her skin and lips were cold and clammy and I feared the worst.

The tears and rage receded enough that I pulled away and saw her goggling at me. The rest of her was still, her eyes staring at me from a skull that wouldn't budge and she whimpered, "I can't move." The helpless and terrified pronouncement lanced the withering balloon of my anger. I kissed her again, pushing my face to hers and tasted the tears. We shared that fear and the sharing was the only thing that kept it from crushing us.

Putting my hands beside her to push myself up, I realized her face was wet from more than tears. The bed, the sheets, her nightgown, were all wet. I looked up to see that the window above the bed had been left open, the rain coming in from outside all night. Cheryl had laid here for the hours between Sophie's abduction and my arrival, unable to move, being covered in rain. She quietly cried, "I can't move. They came and took her and I couldn't do anything. I can't move."

I muttered apologies to her, to Sophie, to the universe. I nearly started to cry as I slid my hands under her knees and shoulders to pick her up. She was a dead weight in my arms. Her head rolled back in a horrid fashion making me think that it might fall off. The victim of a 5.56mm round at a roadblock outside of Al Kut jumped into my brain to join in with the rest of the crazy. I shifted her minuscule weight around in my arms until I got her head to rest on my shoulder.

I don't know if I took her downstairs on autopilot or because I wanted her to be someplace dry. By the time we were at the bottom she had lost consciousness. She wasn't asleep, her eyes still open, but vacant with a tint of fear. I set her on the couch and waited. When I couldn't wait any longer I went upstairs and got her dry clothes, came back down and changed her. It was a bit like changing a mannequin. I tried not to think about it.

In not thinking about it the tears and guilt were gradually supplanted with a cold rage. I couldn't figure out who I was more angry at – me or Verdicchio. I had bet that he wouldn't be willing to upset his orderly life with real violence. I had bet stupidly and bet too much. I imagined the thundering noise of the door, the screaming, maybe Sophie even got desperate enough to call the police.

All that right on his own home turf, not in some quiet car that now seemed parked half a horrid world away.

I suddenly hoped very much that Shaky got home OK.

Chapter 21

"You have to go after her."

It took me a moment to realize Cheryl had spoken. She had managed to turn her eyes to me, but the rest of her remained exactly where I had laid her, motionless.

Like so many times before in my life I said what I thought I was supposed to, my voice sounding detached, like a ventriloquist was projecting it. "Cheryl, things are bad. We need to get you into a hospital or hospice or something, some place where they can take care of you." Not adding, "Until the end." But it hung in the air.

"There's no pain anymore," she said, her eyes returning to the ceiling. The fear that had been there was gone. "I must have peed at some point last night, but I wouldn't know. I was cold and wet, but I can only tell you that because I could hear the rain. But I did feel scared and angry hearing those men come in and hearing Sophie scream as they took her away."

Her eyes came back to me. "You have to go after her."

"No." Cheryl's request ran into the wall of my cold anger. It didn't offer explanation or reason. I had spent so much time trying to avoid thinking about the end that I didn't know what to do now that it was bearing down on us. All I knew was that it was here and I didn't want Cheryl to be alone.

Realizing I had nothing to add I sat on the edge of the coffee table and clasped my hands together over her as if in prayer. I could hear all of the echoes of past arguments with Cheryl in my head, her incensed with my unwillingness or inability to communicate when I had reached this point.

But there wasn't any yelling. I expected her to put her arm around me, but the weight of that familiar comfort never came. The pain of being denied that hurt in a way that her yelling at me never could. It squeezed me and I threatened to pop. I took a rattling breath and tried to put aside my detachment to find something inside myself that felt human. But all I could think about were lost opportunities and wasted moments and how if I were just going to stand here this would just be another one.

"OK." I got up and started rooting around. Behind me Cheryl called my name and asked me what I was doing. I returned a few minutes later with a bundle of clothes and a spare blanket under my arm and the keys to Apartment #3 in my hand. "I'm not going to leave you here with the front door busted open like that." I picked her up and I could have sworn she smiled.

"How are you going to find her?" she asked as I carried her downstairs. I pretended to give that some thought as I moved my feet under me, trying to focus on the mechanics of locomotion rather than Cheryl's weight in my arms.

I shrugged, not sure if she could see or feel my shoulders move, but hoping one would get through. "I'll ask around." I fumbled with the keys to let us into Apartment #3 and managed to do it without dropping her.

"You're going to go after that ugly little man that came around the other day, aren't you?" she asked as I laid her on the couch.

"Hey now," I said, becoming strangely defensive, "Dennis isn't ugly."

Cheryl smiled then with a gleam of her old mischievousness that made me want to smile as well until hers disappeared into a bone-rattling cough. Eventually she came to a dainty finish by clearing her throat. "Sophie said he's ugly."

I repeated the pointless gesture of shrugging as if Dennis' physical attractiveness were somehow a factor in this mess. I realized what it really came down to was, "He's the only person I know in this town."

Worried, she asked, "Is he your friend?"

Another shrug, "I don't know. I'd like to think so. Maybe."

"Are you going to have to hurt him?" She didn't seem terribly concerned about Dennis in asking the question.

"Probably."

To my amazement Cheryl moved, if only just. Slow and tremulous she put her hand on top of mine and gave the tiniest of squeezes. Sympathy pulled down on her mouth and eyes. She pushed that away with a weak smile and said, "Don't do anything I wouldn't do."

In a flash of inexplicable sadism I looked down at her and said, "OK, I'll try not to die."

Laughter burst out of Cheryl. It was long and loud and could have rivaled the craziest of crones or the happiest of children. Despite the cruelty of it all I found myself laughing with her.

After the laughter trailed off I moved my face to hers. I wasn't sure whose tears I tasted as we kissed. "I love you."

"I love you too."

Chapter 22

The morning had long since died, but it hadn't gotten late enough in the day yet for the Mondiale to be open. I found a perch where I could watch the bar through the crowds of daytrippers for awhile, trying to detect if there was any trouble and trying to come up with some sort of plan. The bar was dark and empty and I knew I should be grateful for that. Most likely Dennis was the only one inside getting ready for his nightly business. But part of me regretted its bright lights weren't on to show off its polished brass and warm wood with a crazy local or three shouting at the TV over some soccer match.

I crossed the stream of daytrippers, tried my luck on the door and found it unlocked. Knowing that anyone inside could see me through the windows, I closed my eyes and took a deep breath, then pushed through.

A bell rang over my head as I came in filling the Mondiale with a high, tinny sound. The haji boy, cleaning a table across the room, saw me enter. By the look he gave me he must have known I was trouble. I returned his gaze with a well-practiced threatening glare and he disappeared into the back.

Dennis rose up from behind the bar. He was clearly prepared to expel some tourist who had mistakenly wandered in, but realizing it was me his eyes flipped to another setting. He said, "G'day," his tone flat.

"No," I replied, crossing the short distance to the bar, "it's not."

"Surprised to see you." He picked up a glass and began cleaning it like he was about to offer me a

One Sore Rib

drink. He didn't.

"Why's that?" Dennis had always struck me as someone it would be very difficult to surprise.

He twisted the glass with one hand, carefully polishing its surface with the rag in his other. "Verdicchio tipped the ecilops. They were meant to be waiting for you at the train station." I thought about the fisherman and his boat again, but didn't see a reason to share that with Dennis.

"Where is she?" I didn't bother to threaten him. My voice sounded hollow in the cavern of Mondiale.

"None of your business, mate. Whatever playtime the two of you had is long gone past and you should see to your other duties." Surprisingly, I found what Dennis was implying to be hurtful. I had hoped he thought better of me.

He must have read that in my face because his own softened. He put his hands flat on the bar and leaned forward in the closest thing Dennis had to a friendly manner. "You don't have much time left, mate. None of us do. Go home, be with your wife, and wait for the end."

With a twinge of sympathy I realized that's what Dennis had been doing here in Venice. Whatever had brought him here, whatever kept Dennis trapped here, it had him living for whatever quiet moments of happiness he could find in between doing Verdicchio's bidding. He was biding time until the end. So that's when I pinned his hand to the bar with the knife.

I swung the KA-BAR up and around fast enough and hard enough to embed the first few inches of it in the soft wood through the back of his palm. He didn't do anything for a second other than widen his eyes in surprise. Then he started screaming bloody murder. I held the blade in place as he danced and yelled, threatening me and taking wild swings. But his reach wasn't good enough to get at me and mine was good enough to keep him stuck.

When the first phase of his panicked and pained dance had slowed down I leaned in close. "Where is she?"

Dennis' eyes, normally clear and calm, were bloodshot and angry as anything I've ever seen as he screamed back. He called me a litany of nasty things, most of which I didn't recognize. I let him blow himself out, then asked again, "Where is she?"

Dennis replied with a rather sturdy, "Fuck you." He leaned in with what I believed to be an equally firm intention of biting the hand I was using to keep the knife in place.

Rather than back off or release the handle I let him get closer and asked, "Tell me you're not the Beast."

Dennis' confusion stopped him just a few inches short of sinking incisors into my knuckles. Instead it caused him to say, "Wha?"

I stayed there, one hand on the knife grip, the other on its pommel, and said, "Tell me you're not the Beast."

Anger started back into Dennis' eyes as he gritted his teeth like he was sharpening them to rend red meat from me. "What the Hell are you on about?"

I put the weight of my elbow on the bar. "I told you about the Beast and his Master. And we both know Verdicchio's the Master of this place." I got close enough that I could have kissed him. "Tell me you're not the Beast."

The anger drained out of Dennis as he began to comprehend what I was saying. Like any good soldier, though, he gave it one last, "Fuck you."

"Tell me, Dennis. I really need to hear that right now." My free hand holding the wrist of his trapped arm, Dennis leaned his forehead down to the bar and banged its surface four times, rhythmically, each one slower than the last. Then he told me.

I pulled the knife out of the bar and said, "Thanks."

Dennis examined his wounded hand, estimating the damage. Almost absently he said to me, "He'll know you're coming."

I wiped the blood off the knife with a bar towel. "No, he won't. But you can tell him if you want."

Dennis' gaze snapped up from his hand, angry again, now at the situation I'd put him in. "You bloody drongo, you've killed us all."

"Maybe so," I said, slipping the KA-BAR back into its sheath.

Chapter 23

It made sense where Verdicchio took her. If you're taking a screaming or unconscious woman through someplace as small and crowded as Venice, you aren't going to want to take her far. If it were anywhere else you could stick her in a trunk and get a reasonable distance, but there are no cars in Venice.

What Venice did have was innumerable palazzos, tiny palaces that had served as grand residential estates back in the island's glory days. Most, however, had long since been converted to hotels, warehouses, office space, or apartment buildings. The one Verdicchio had picked was large by Venetian standards but little more than a big townhouse by American ones. It was a three-story box, but a beautiful box I had to admit. With a red-pink facade to match the terracotta roof, its three levels were dotted with windows whose peaked arches reminded me of a mosque. It sat right on the canal, a stone's throw away from a bridge so if a retreat became necessary Verdicchio could get out by land or sea.

I got all this by just walking by the place on the opposite side of the canal, pretending to be any other tourist, if a smelly and bedraggled one. Peering into the shops on my side of the water, I spotted a walking tour establishment that had a few computers on counter-tops. Striding in I played the boorish American to the hilt, talking too fast to be understood and loud enough to be really annoying. The young man who tried to help me was impressively patient for an Italian. I kept at it until I could sense his exasperation rising, then gestured to one of the computers, asking to use it. He gratefully indicated for

One Sore Rib

me to go ahead and do that.

An online computer gave me access to maps, records, satellite photos, all the things a growing boy needs to plan an assault. Now that I had the palazzo plotted and the internet, I could find out more in a few minutes than I could in hours of physical reconnaissance. Searching by address I quickly found beautiful images of the building just out the shop window. More important to me, though, was that it had a dozen ground-floor entrances, one or two balconies on each side, an open courtyard in the middle, and at least one rooftop access point.

It ended up that the building, like a lot of palazzos in Venice, was semi-famous. As such I was able to locate floor plans. These showed the insides to be mostly a honeycomb of small rooms and tight spaces with a few long hallways and banquet rooms. It was typically used as a hotel/event hall, so Verdicchio must have rented the whole place and cleared it for his personal use on this special occasion.

Deep in thought, I barely registered one of the shop girls as she came over to me. I shooed her away, but could tell by the way she whispered to a fellow employee my time on the computer was running out. And I desperately wanted more.

After gathering what information I could I was forced to conclude that getting in and out with Sophie was going to be impossible. The roof wasn't reachable without access to one of the neighboring buildings. My short walk-by had told me that most of the windows had been closed against the late October cold. And while it was unlikely that Verdicchio's crew had a picture of me it wasn't impossible and they surely, at a minimum, had a rough description. Although, I rationalized, that clean-cut man probably bore little resemblance to the scruffy loner sitting at this computer.

However, as the tour shop employees congregated near the back, whispering and casting glances in my direction, I hit on something. I hadn't seen it from the opposite side of the canal, but in the front part, on the first floor of the palazzo, was a coffee shop. A public coffee shop. While Verdicchio might have the rest of his palace cordoned off, he'd probably have a mutiny on his hands if he tried to keep his thugs away from their allotment of espresso.

I took what little time I had left to try and memorize as much of the floor plans as I could, focusing on stairwells and places Verdicchio might have stowed Sophie. The shop boy I had originally spoken to began walking over to me, so I finished up and made placating and apologetic noises and gestures as I left. If I hadn't been on my way to face certain danger I might have felt ruffled by the clerks' stares. Nobody does pissy like the Italians.

I started up the bridge to the palazzo's side of the canal, trying to mix in with the crowd, keeping my face hidden in my hood. I stopped at the apex of the bridge and watched boats go by, the air filled with a faint puttering of motors and the chatter of the many languaged tourists. I wished for a pair of binoculars, but then that grew into a laundry list of things I wanted – weapons, thermo-imaging, a helicopter, my old squad. I strangled that chain of thought like the snake it was before it got too big or too long. Wishing for things I couldn't have would only keep me from acting.

A brisk march off the bridge put me into the thick of the daytrippers and I moved along in that stream of people towards the palazzo. Its balconies were empty, its windows shuttered, and in the gray of that morning it managed to appear uninviting even with its bright facade. Much to my relief the small café was open with chairs lined up out front, facing the canal.

The increasing cold may not have forced the proprietor to close the two sets of ancient glass and wood double doors that made the cafe's entrance, but it did mean a lot more demand for hot beverages. People moved briskly in and out. None of them took to-go cups. Each customer walked in, ordered, waited for the minute it took to receive their beverage, housed in a tiny porcelain cup. They then drank it quickly and departed, all with a neat efficiency brought on by years of practice.

I watched this from the edge of the canal, leaning against a striped mooring pole, hoping I was inconspicuous. Minutes of observation revealed that while most people quickly moved in and out, there were some who sat at small tables inside, sipping their drinks and taking their time. Most of these were marked by their gray hair as old pensioners, whiling away whatever years they had left. However, two near a door in the back could have been part of Verdicchio's crew.

One was an oval-faced man close to my age with a box haircut, wearing a black turtleneck with brown trousers. He was arguing over the sugar with an older man whose head was thick with bushy hair that came down to the collar of his striped shirt. Using a bit of mental cartography I figured the door they were near was the one that went from the café to the palazzo proper.

I pushed off the pole and started away from the cafe, not wanting to stay too long and possibly draw attention to myself. The palazzo had two streets going down on either side, so I ducked down one hoping to do a walk-around. I was grateful to find that the building didn't have anyone stationed outside the doors along the narrow cobbled streets, but was disappointed to find it didn't have a back entrance. The rear of the building shared its wall with a series of retail shops. I briefly considered trying to break through the common wall from one of the stores. Like most of the ideas I was coming up with, though, I quickly dismissed it as absurd.

Other than locked and shuttered doors and windows into the palazzo, the only passage I found was an alley that led to the building's courtyard. Judging by the wheeled, gray-steel trash bin there, it was primarily used for garbage collection. On the alley wall next to it was what appeared to be a circuit breaker box. Seeing it unattended, I just shook my head. Then I headed back to the retail stores.

In a salon I bought an over-sized can of hairspray and some incense. From a convenience store across the way I picked up some tape, a lighter, and a small screwdriver. The hardest part, it ended up, was finding a place with some privacy. After scouring the sestieri for what felt like an infuriating eternity I found a public toilet. I locked the stall and took care of my first priority – relieving myself.

That mission accomplished I taped a stick of incense to the can of hairspray. I made sure the tip of it was parallel to the can's nozzle, but reaching out beyond the top almost to the stick's full length. Hiding the can under my jacket I headed out, humming the theme song to *M*A*S*H*.

Back at the alley I discovered to my amazement that the small alley was still unguarded. I verified that I wasn't being watched, then took out the screwdriver and broke the tiny lock off the breaker box. I verified there was enough room, then placed the hairspray can inside and used the lighter to light the incense stick.

I couldn't help close my eyes and pray a little

when I broke off the aerosol's plunger cap – the contents began to leak almost immediately and this was the moment of greatest danger. If my idea worked right, the incense would function as a slow fuse and burn down, eventually igniting the stream of hairspray when it filled the contained space and, hopefully, cause a fire in the box. If I was lucky it might knock out the power to the palazzo.

If I was wrong, it might just blow up in my face. In that moment, even with everything else going on, the idea of this happening worried me the most. Being found blind and handless in Verdicchio's backyard was just too embarrassing to stomach.

The incense continued to burn without blowing me up so I slapped the box door shut and walked back around to the café. I strode inside and got shoulder to shoulder with the other dozen patrons at the counter. The place was shallow but wide, taking up the front section of the palazzo's first floor. The interior was made up of the same glass, wood trim, amber paint, and gild work as its doors. The counter was marble topped with the curved display case that you might find in any deli.

I passed the seconds in line by eyeing the pastries underneath it. They looked delicious, which made me realize I hadn't eaten in a long time. My stomach growled into life. A plain young woman snapped at me from behind the bar and I said, "Un café," and pointed to a pastry. Both came up quickly. I grabbed them and pushed through the crowd to sit at a small wooden table. My chair creaked under my weight and the corrosion brought on by years of close proximity to the canal's brine.

Despite everything I ate with great relish, trying to keep from pushing the entire pastry into my mouth at once. To slow myself down I focused on rolling a few napkins in non-dairy creamer. I went about this, biting, chewing, rolling, until I noticed the two men by the door glancing in my direction between whispers. I angled my face away from them, staring out through the café entrance to the canal, hoping they hadn't recognized me.

Before I found out if they had though, I was saved by the distant sound of thunder. To me, it was as if someone had fired off a howitzer and I was hearing the echo bounce back from mountains. As the lights in the café flickered, Verdicchio's men shoved and pushed their way through the crowd to get outside and investigate the noise.

I realized the can must have exploded under its own pressure. And with quite a nice bang too. In that high, thin valley of an alley it must have thrown all the noise up and out.

Following in the wake of the gangsters everyone else moved to the doors, some checking the sky for rain. To the café staff's credit no one came out from behind the counter, but they were distracted enough that not one noticed as I lit the bundle of napkins on fire. The creamer went up so fast it singed my hand as I dropped it into a trashcan. I strolled away in what I hoped was a casual manner.

Whatever fears I had about the stupidity of this venture were briefly eclipsed by malicious glee when smoke began to billow out. The faces of the coffee crew went from casual Italian disdain to frenetic panic. One beanpole of a young man nearly jumped over the counter. With everyone distracted I made my way to the back of the café, pushed the screwdriver into the door's lock and slipped into the palazzo.

For a moment I thought I had walked into a closet. There were no lights or windows. After my eyes adjusted to the dimness I could see it was a small entry room with a sliver of daylight coming from a hallway at the other

One Sore Rib

end. More importantly voices were coming down the hall's wood-paneled floor.

Quickly searching for an exit I saw that there was a set of stairs going up next to where the hallway joined the entryway and a door to my immediate right. I tried the door's knob and breathed a sigh of relief that it was unlocked. That relief was replaced with the image of a battalion of Verdicchio's goons standing on the other side. I slipped through the door anyway.

No one was there. The room on the other side was a large utility closet lit by a high, small window on the opposite wall. It cast dim light on shelves stacked with various paint cans and cleaning agents.

I focused my attention on closing the door quietly as the voices coming down the hall became louder. The doorknob had a dimpled feel to it, like old pig iron, and creaked and groaned incredibly loudly as I tried to click it shut. Pulling the door into place, breath catching in my chest, I looked down to see the reason it was making this much noise – the knob could have been something out of the Victorian age. It probably hadn't been greased since the last World War. It also had a keyhole you could drive a truck through. I bent at the knees to peek through it.

From that vantage point the two men coming down the hallway were nothing but silhouettes. Their voices carried well because they were arguing in a very animated way. Bracing myself against the door I watched as they stopped just short of the outer door I had just come through. One man threw his hands up, exclaiming something I didn't understand as the other gestured for him to stay. The first man pulled his hands out of the air and grabbed the doorknob, snapping it open as if in protest. When the smoke and noise came out of the café he dove into the light, leaving his companion standing in the hall and yelling after him. He cursed and closed the door, leaving me with only an afterimage of him.

I was trapped. The closet I was in had no exit other than passed the man who was standing in the hall. The window was far too small for an escape and would only lead outside. Knowing the longer I remained in here the greater the chance of being caught, I did the only thing I could think of. I threw the door open. The light coming from the window behind me, as dim as it was, caused him to blink in surprise. I didn't give him a chance to think. I hit him as hard as I could as fast as I could where I thought it would hurt him the most. He went down like a sack of potatoes that I dragged back into the closet.

Inside I could see he was young, younger than the Kid, a gap-toothed child with his brown haircut into a bowl and wearing an outfit that made him look like a priest. With his butt on the floor I pinned his head and shoulders to the wall with one hand on his throat and brought him back to cognizance by slapping him. Coming back to life, his eyes bulged and he started to struggle. I put a stop to that by cracking his head on the wall and increasing the tension around his throat. His expression changed from alarmed to pleading and I knew I had his attention. I asked, "Where's Sophie?"

The answers that came out of his mouth weren't ones I understood so I choked him harder, this time so hard his eyes went in different directions. I had to let go of his neck when an anger I didn't realize I had been holding onto came up in a rush so strong that it made me want to kill him. Instead I gave him a good shake and asked again, "Where's Sophie?"

An expression came into his eyes that was afraid and soft enough to belong to a dog. He didn't speak, just pointed a single finger up towards the ceiling of the closet. The anger was gone, being replaced with pity. I

One Sore Rib

drove that out of me by tightening my grip and asking, "Verdicchio?" His finger, still pointing, moved up and down, emphasizing the upstairs. "Where?" His hand blossomed from one finger to three. "Third floor," I said and he nodded though I'm pretty sure he didn't know what I was saying.

I reached out my left hand, found something heavy, and cracked him on the temple with it. His head snapped to the right with a sickening thud.

I peeked through the keyhole to make sure the hallway was clear. Through its narrow scope I saw the foyer was still empty, but I thought I heard more voices. I couldn't tell if it was that or paranoia droning in my head. Either way it was good motivation to move fast so I shot out of the door, closed it behind me and headed for the stairs.

I took them two at a time, swinging my shoulders and arms like pistons. When I ran into a man descending the stairs I drove my fist up and out into his solar plexus, collapsing him nearly before we saw each other. I grabbed his shoulders as he fell towards me, swinging him around and then releasing him to fall down the stairs.

At the top I restrained myself long enough to try peering through the keyhole of the door there, but nothing doing. I gripped the knob, breathed as calm as I could, holding it as I cracked open the door to peek through. Bright light poured out from a large empty hall. I stepped in, sticking close to the wall near the door as if I might blend in with the wallpaper.

I realized the hall wasn't a passage but some kind of exhibit room, with three glass patio doors that formed its southern wall letting in an almost blinding amount of light. Staggered on both sides of the room at regular intervals were small columns that terminated at chest height, each with a tiny cherub on top. The minuscule, babyish angels stared at each other and around the room with playfully gleeful expressions set there by the sculptor.

The room had several exits besides the glass doors. I walked around, trying to surreptitiously see down each one, feeling a bit like a Scooby-Doo character as I peeked my head around the frames. One hallway that let off the room was formed by a series of open, tall glass doors that telescoped out to where another angel statue stood at a T in the hallway. I took that as a sign and went down it.

To the statue's right the hallway practically vomited with color, all of the walls covered in swirls that belonged more in a children's book than in this place. It did make the fat man in the dark suit easy to spot though. Standing in front of a closed door he gazed out through tall windows opposite him in the hard way of a sentinel. He appeared to be one of the few men here who had the discipline not to have left his post. That meant whatever he was guarding was important.

There was nothing between me and him, so I tore ass down the hallway, hitting him at full speed just as he rotated his bulk to see me. A credit to his girth, his feet barely left the ground as I slammed into him, but he did fall down. One angry eye glared out from behind his askew sunglasses before I grabbed him by his collar and pummeled him into submission. After he stopped struggling, I gulped heaps of air and tried to slow my heartbeat. Between the rhythms of my internal combustion I thought I could hear Verdicchio's voice at the door.

I wasn't sure what I was going to find, only that I wanted to find Sophie and get out. Out on the streets we might find the protection of the masses and just enough time to grab Cheryl and get out of town. I pushed open the doors with a recklessness born out of that foolish

One Sore Rib

hope.

To my left Sophie was tied to the headboard of a bed with sheets of white and red. Verdicchio stood to the right, wrapped in linens, something out of a frat boy's toga party. He was leering at Sophie like a man who was about to start or had just finished something. As he faced me I could see he had a cigarette in one hand and pruning shears in the other.

Recognizing me, his expression went from anger to surprise. He dropped the shears and went for the bed stand next to him. I went for Verdicchio.

Old age and guile might beat youth and enthusiasm most of the time, but not in a race across the room to a bed stand with a loaded revolver in it. Verdicchio had the drawer open by the time I got to him. I pushed him over the stand and smashed him into the wall. The bed stand, its lamp, Verdicchio, and the pistol all flew into the air and crashed to the floor. I gave him a good kick to make sure he didn't reach for the weapon, then bent down to pick it up along with the shears. The shears were sticky with blood.

Without thinking I leaned forward and cut Sophie's hands free, my mind blocking out the blood. It was the spittle and sweat covered ball gag in her mouth that snapped me out of it, thinking of her screaming and pulling against the headboard.

I turned my head to Verdicchio to find him sitting up, his expression nothing but contempt. The incomprehension I felt must have been all over me. He casually stood and picked up his cigarette as if he was waiting for me to take his order.

"What the fuck did you do?" With the sheets I couldn't tell how he had cut her. And while I was grateful for that, I couldn't even begin to understand why he had.

"You may have her." Verdicchio brushed us away

with his hand. "I've damaged her in a way that you'll never be able to enjoy her again." He took a drag from the cigarette. "If you run now you might be able to get out before others arrive."

I felt my body turn to him fully then, set upon an inexorable course. I found all the rage that I thought I'd left in the first floor closet. It mixed with a strange calm that unsettled Verdicchio more than being smashed into the wall had. But he didn't back down or run away, just kept smoking that cigarette as I closed the distance between us. I blinked a few times, feeling empty-headed and certain.

"I've decided," I said, my voice sounding like it was coming from somewhere else, "the world would be a better place without you in it."

I dropped the pistol and shears, hearing them both bounce off the floor and echo in the large room. I latched my hands around Verdicchio's throat, digging my fingernails in and crushing everything I could. He struggled and scratched like you'd expect from a first class bastard. After a few minutes he had flayed most of the skin off my forearms and hands, but I just kept squeezing until I saw the light go out of his eyes. I kept squeezing until his tongue popped out and I felt his windpipe collapse under the pressure.

I opened my hands and he fell to the floor like a deboned fish. I turned back to the bed to find Sophie was now standing next to it in blood stained sheets. The ball gag was gone. She was rubbing tears and sweat out of her eyes with the root of her palm, looking as vacant as I felt. Having watched Verdicchio die didn't seem to affect her, one way or another.

I wanted to say something, comfort her or ask (stupidly) if she was OK. Before I could I heard footsteps beyond the room's door, heavy and urgent feet moving this way. I scrambled to find the revolver as Sophie listlessly shuffled and staggered, maybe searching for her own lost thing.

Coming up with the pistol I found Sophie between me and the exit. Pointing the revolved at the door meant pointing it at her so I yelled, "Sophie, get out of the way!"

She didn't move. I urgently repeated myself. She was still standing there as the first two men came through.

The one on the left was another old-timer dressed in casual Italian wear with practical shoes that wouldn't slip in a puddle of blood. The other was a boy trying to dress the part of a Mafioso, a nice suit that he barely filled out, too much room around the collar showing a neck that supported a tall, thin head with dark, spindly hair. I'll remember what he looked like for the rest of my life. Because that's when Sophie stabbed him in the neck with the curved beak of the pruning shears.

As the boy fell back spouting blood and trying to scream through all that wet, the old-timer made a grab for Sophie. She went for his eyes. The two of them became a blur of his waving hands and the metallic glint of Sophie's blades. After a few seconds of her cutting, stabbing, and snapping at him he ran out of the room screaming, leaving behind a few flaps of skin on the floor.

With the boy dying at her feet and the echo of the old-timer's screams coming from the hall Sophie rotated her head, giving me an empty gaze over her shoulder. I only saw one eye, the other being covered by her sweat soaked hair. But whatever was in that eye was unfathomable to me, blank and endless. Then, shears in hand, she walked out of the room on a cloud of the same eerie quiet she had been inhabiting since getting off the bed.

I followed her. She didn't take the same path down

as I took up, so I hoped she was taking us to a direct exit. We didn't even get down the first flight of stairs before more footsteps signaled more trouble. Not sure where the noise was coming from, I kept the revolver out and ready, pointing it past Sophie as I thought the footsteps might be coming from downstairs.

They were. The first of what could have been a dozen men whipped around the bend in the stairwell. He came to a sliding halt aided by pinwheeling arms, causing him to collide with the others behind him. With his face right in the gun sight I thought the threat of a bullet was making him reconsider his up-stairs offensive. But he wasn't looking at me.

He was looking at Sophie. All of them were. They were staring at her as if she were some kind of specter, eyes wide and startled like she had just walked out of one of grandma's superstitions. Sophie raised her hands like a priest at the altar and the shears' blades clicked open, spattering the white walls with droplets of blood.

The crowd of men below her began to back away slowly. She moved into the empty space they left behind, inch-by-inch.

Over the course of the remaining two flights of stairs the crowd behind the front man dissolved into the ether, abandoning the poor guy at any given opportunity. By the time we got to the bottom I had his wide nose and misshaped head memorized. I had never taken my eyes off him and he had never looked away from Sophie. By the time he stumbled backward onto the first floor he was completely alone. My feet hit the same floor and he seemed to realize I was there. As if that had broken the spell his eyes darted from Sophie to me and back again. Then he turned and ran, his feet clopping down the hallway as fast as they could carry him.

One Sore Rib

Before we stepped outside I stuck the revolver in my waistband, took off the hoodie and wrapped Sophie in it. Once I had covered her as best I could I picked her up and went.

It was a very long walk back to the apartment. But even with me looking bearded, dark-eyed, pale, and haggard, carrying a woman wrapped in white, black, and red, we didn't attract much attention. I suppose people might have thought we were some kind of performance art.

Once at the apartment I was incredibly grateful that I'd moved Cheryl to the second floor. I don't think I could have made it to the third. I had to set Sophie down in order to get my keys out. She slipped from my arms to her feet without a word, but snatched the keys from me when I had them in hand. She quickly unlocked the door and I thought I almost saw her smile as she pushed it open and went in. I nearly collapsed from relief at that, feeling all of the fatigue and pain from the last two days.

When I heard Sophie's wail from inside I knew Cheryl was dead. I almost didn't follow her in, but I couldn't. I had to see. It was as if gravity had changed and the floor tilted and I slid in. She was there on the couch like she had been a dozen times before, but different, something indefinable having left.

I knew I should run. One of Verdicchio's boys would eventually find the courage to come after us, or police would be asking hospital staff about Dennis' hand, or be connecting me to Shaky in Marghera. I knew they were coming, that I should run.

I cried anyway.

= = =

Thank you for reading.
Please review this book. Reviews help others find New Pulp Press and inspire us to keep providing these marvelous tales.

If you would like to be put on our email list to receive updates on new releases, contests, and promotions, please go to NewPulpPress.com and sign up.

About the Author

Matthew C. McLean is a native of Kansas City who has since lived all across the United States. He currently resides with his wife in North Carolina. To learn more visit http://www.MatthewCMcLean.com

NewPulpPress.com

Made in the USA
Lexington, KY
01 October 2017